David Aldred is a fantasy author from Ashton-under-Lyne. A lifelong fan of the genre, he grew up immersed in the worlds of *The Lord of the Rings* and *Harry Potter*, which inspired him to create his own epic tales.

His debut novel is the first in a gripping five-book fantasy series that blends magic, adventure and rich storytelling. When he isn't writing, he enjoys drawing, exploring mythology and diving deep into world-building.

To my three children, Alby, Heidi and Leonard — the inspirations behind the characters of Eryndal, Soren and Roland. You inspire me to be better every day.

David Aldred

ERYNDAL AND THE KINGDOM OF RELDAD: THE SERPENTS TALE

AUSTIN MACAULEY PUBLISHERS
LONDON · CAMBRIDGE · NEW YORK · SHARJAH

Copyright © David Aldred 2025

The right of David Aldred to be identified as author of this work has been asserted by the author in accordance with sections 77 and 78 of the Copyright, Designs and Patents Act 1988.

All rights reserved. No part of this publication may be reproduced, stored in a retrieval system, or transmitted in any form or by any means, electronic, mechanical, photocopying, recording, or otherwise, without the prior permission of the publishers.

Any person who commits any unauthorised act in relation to this publication may be liable to criminal prosecution and civil claims for damages.

This is a work of fiction. Names, characters, businesses, places, events, locales, and incidents are either the products of the author's imagination or used in a fictitious manner. Any resemblance to actual persons, living or dead, or actual events is purely coincidental.

A CIP catalogue record for this title is available from the British Library.

ISBN 9781037105937 (Paperback)
ISBN 9781037105944 (ePub e-book)

www.austinmacauley.com

First Published 2025
Austin Macauley Publishers Ltd®
1 Canada Square
Canary Wharf
London
E14 5AA

Chapter 1
Reldad, The Heart of Magic

Reldad was a land unlike any other; a realm where the forces of nature and the ancient magics of the world blended seamlessly. It was a land where the very elements of earth, air, fire, and water danced in harmony, as though guided by an unseen hand—one that wove the very fabric of life. The whisper of the wind could carry the voice of the gods themselves, while the mountains, towering and majestic, hummed with the power of forgotten legends. Every inch of Reldad seemed to pulse with the heartbeat of magic, from the soaring peaks to the deepest caverns, as though the land itself were alive, a living entity with memories older than time itself.

The kingdom stretched far and wide, a vast expanse that touched every corner of the world, a realm of beauty and danger, of wonders unseen by those outside its borders. To the uninitiated, Reldad appeared as a paradise, a land bathed in the soft glow of magic and the warmth of sun-dappled forests. But those who dared to explore it soon learned that Reldad was no easy place to tame. It was not a realm that could be subdued or conquered by force alone. The land demanded respect, and those who underestimated its power would quickly discover its capacity for wrath.

The people of Reldad, wise and ancient, knew this truth well. Every stone underfoot, every gust of wind that swept across the plains, and every droplet of water that fell from the sky seemed to carry with it an ancient memory. It was said that the very soil of Reldad remembered the footsteps of the gods—those divine beings who had once walked among the earth, leaving behind a trail of power and knowledge that still echoed through the ages. Travellers, when they walked through the fertile lands of Reldad, often whispered that the soil underfoot was warm to the touch, imbued with a deep, almost sacred energy that connected them to something greater than themselves.

If one listened closely enough, the wind would carry more than just the scent of flowers or the soft murmur of a distant stream—it would carry the voices of the gods, faint whispers of laughter, sorrow, and power. These were the remnants of an ancient time when the gods had walked freely among mortals, shaping the world with their will. Some believed that if one stood in the right place at the right time, they might even hear a god's voice speaking directly into their soul. Others said that the land itself was haunted by the spirits of those who had fallen from grace, their presence woven into the fabric of the world.

But whatever the truth of these whispers, one thing was certain: Reldad was alive; not merely a stretch of land but a living, breathing entity that could not be ignored. Its people, who lived among its hills and forests, understood this well. They knew that the land demanded not only reverence but caution. Those who took its gifts for granted, who treated the earth as something to be owned or controlled, were often met with fierce retribution. Reldad was no ordinary kingdom, and its magic was not something to be used lightly.

The geography of Reldad mirrored the diversity of its people, a reflection of the many cultures, races, and beings that called the kingdom home. At the northern edge of Reldad lay the awe-inspiring expanse of the **Varnor Mountains**, their jagged peaks eternally cloaked in snow and ice. Stretching across the northern horizon, these frozen titans formed a natural barrier between the kingdom and the unknown lands beyond. Treacherous and beautiful, the mountains were alive with biting winds and shimmering glaciers that caught the light of the northern sun. Yet amidst this frozen wilderness, there was a remarkable anomaly—a sheltered plateau that escaped the grip of snow and ice.

Here, overlooking the vast and restless **Bershian Sea**, lay a hidden refuge of verdant beauty. This temperate enclave, warmed by mysterious geothermal springs, was home to the **Citadel of Kings and Queens, Elderion Citadel**. The citadel, an architectural marvel of silver stone and ancient craftsmanship, rose proudly above the cliffs, its towers catching the salt-laden winds from the sea. From this vantage point, rulers of Reldad had long watched over their kingdom and beyond, the Bershian Sea stretching endlessly before them. The citadel stood as both a sanctuary and a seat of power, its unique location a symbol of the unity and resilience of the realm, even in the face of nature's harshest elements.

To the east, the Reldadan Mountains rose like a wall of stone, their jagged peaks scraping the heavens themselves. These mountains were a land of mystery, their caves and valleys home to creatures as old as time, some believed to be the remnants of an age before the gods. The mountain ranges were rumoured to contain hidden sanctuaries where great sorcerers once studied the arcane arts, and where now only the bravest adventurers dared venture. At the summit of the Reldadan Mountains, where the air grew thin and cold, the wind carried whispers of ancient power, and the very rocks seemed to pulse with untapped energy.

Also in the east, the Sea of Sirrath gleamed under the golden light of the sun. Its waters were deep and treacherous, hiding ancient secrets and forgotten treasures beneath its dark, glassy surface. The sea stretched for miles, its tides forever shifting, as though the very ocean itself were alive and capable of harbouring both beauty and danger in equal measure. Sailors who ventured too far out into the Sirrath returned with wild tales—stories of ghostly ships that appeared out of nowhere and vanished just as quickly, of glowing underwater cities lost to time, and of a mysterious creature they called The Watcher.

The Watcher, some said, was a guardian of the sea, a massive being of unknowable form that lived in the depths of the ocean, keeping watch over the secrets buried there. Those who claimed to have seen The Watcher spoke of its glowing eyes that gleamed with an eerie light, watching from the abyss. Sailors who encountered it often spoke of a deep, unsettling feeling—a sense of being watched, of being caught in the gaze of something ancient and powerful. Some believed that those who saw The Watcher would be marked for a great change, their destinies altered forever. Others whispered that the creature was a harbinger of doom, a sign that the world was on the brink of great calamity.

To the south, lay the Verdant Wilds, an endless expanse of enchanted forests, alive with magic and teeming with creatures both fair and foul. The trees here were ancient, their trunks towering high above the ground, their branches twisting and intertwining to form canopies so thick that sunlight barely touched the forest floor. The Verdant Wilds were home to some of Reldad's oldest and most secretive inhabitants: the elves, fae, and gnomes. These creatures were said to have walked the world since its earliest days, their connection to the land as deep as the roots of the great trees that grew there. The forests themselves were alive with magic, and it was said that the rivers that wound through the Wilds were not merely made of water but of pure, unshaped magic, coursing through the land like the blood of the earth itself.

To the west, the Blackwater Marshes lay in shadow, a land of stagnant waters and thick mists, where light seldom penetrated the dense fog that clung to the earth like a living thing. The marshes were riddled with dangerous sinkholes, sudden drops that could swallow a man whole, and treacherous quicksand that could pull a person under in a matter of seconds. The air was thick with the scent of decay and damp earth, and the silence was broken only by the occasional croak of a distant frog or the flutter of wings as strange, unseen creatures passed overhead.

But it was not just the land that was dangerous here. The Blackwater Marshes were home to ancient spirits—beings of shadow and mist that had once been mortal but were now bound to the land by ancient curses. These spirits, some said, were the remnants of a forgotten order that once sought to dominate all magic in Reldad, bending the forces of nature to their will. But the order had long since been destroyed, their power shattered, leaving only the restless ghosts of their former selves behind. And though they no longer had bodies, their influence lingered, a dark, insidious presence that haunted the marshes.

And between these extremes—the soaring peaks of the north and the mysterious swamps of the west—lay a kingdom of cities, forests, and plains, connected by roads paved with ancient magic. These roads shimmered faintly under the light of the moon; their enchantments woven into the very stones that formed their paths. The roads were alive with magic, their very existence a testament to the power of the old world. It was said that the roads were imbued with the power to ward off darkness and to guide lost travellers home. Even when night fell and the land grew cold and dangerous, the roads remained lit by an ethereal glow, their magic preventing the shadows from creeping in too far.

But despite the protective magic woven into the roads, they were not without their dangers. Bandits roamed the highways, rogue beasts from the deep forests prowled at the edges, and sometimes, there were even rogue sorcerers—those who had become corrupted by the very magic they sought to control. These dark practitioners were feared above all else, for their power could warp the land itself, turning a peaceful glade into a twisted nightmare of shadow and flame.

And yet, despite these dangers, the roads remained the lifeblood of Reldad. They were the veins through which the kingdom's commerce, knowledge, and magic flowed, connecting the farthest reaches of the land with the bustling heart of the kingdom's cities. In Reldad, no matter where you went, magic was always with you. Whether it was the magic of the land or the magic of the people, it was a force that could heal and destroy, bind and free, give and take away. It was the very essence of Reldad, and it coursed through the kingdom like the blood in its veins.

The Eternal Land

At the heart of Reldad, where the forces of nature and the mystical energies of the world met in perfect harmony, lay the floating city of Aetherion—a place that defied the very laws of nature. Suspended between the heavens and the earth, it was a marvel of magic and architecture, a city held aloft by ancient spells and the will of the gods themselves. To the untrained eye, Aetherion appeared as a dream made manifest—a shimmering mass of stone, crystal, and magic that floated effortlessly in the sky, tethered to the ground below by glowing chains of ethereal energy. Its towers were immense, constructed from gleaming crystals that sparkled in the sunlight like diamonds. These towers reached towards the heavens, their surfaces refracting sunlight into a dazzling array of rainbows that painted the skies above the city and the surrounding countryside. It was as though the city itself were a living beacon, calling out to the world below.

Aetherion's streets pulsed with energy, as though the city were not merely a collection of stone and crystal, but a living, breathing entity. Magic flowed through the city's veins as rivers of power ran along its thoroughfares, glowing like molten streams of liquid light. This magic powered everything in Aetherion—from the floating lanterns that lit the streets to the massive aerial platforms that transported goods and people from one place to another. These platforms were not bound by gravity; they hovered effortlessly in the air, carried by the enchantments woven into the very fabric of the city. The air itself was thick with the scent of spellcraft—a heady mixture of ozone, burnt herbs, and something faintly metallic, the unmistakable fragrance of magic at work. To walk the streets of Aetherion was to feel as though one were walking through a dream where the very laws of reality bent and shifted at will.

Scholars, wizards, and sorcerers from all corners of Reldad flocked to Aetherion, drawn by the promise of knowledge and the allure of its magical energies. At the heart of the city stood the Magisterium, the council of the most powerful sorcerers in the land. The Magisterium was more than just a gathering of wise men and women; it was the beating heart of magical research and governance in Reldad. Within the grand halls of the Magisterium, debates raged endlessly about the nature of magic, its uses and abuses, its limits and its dangers. The magisters, clad in robes woven from threads of pure starlight, were both revered and feared by the people of Reldad. Their power was unmatched, and it was said that a single word from a magister could reshape reality itself. Yet, such power was seldom used lightly. The magisters preferred to remain in the shadows of their grand halls, guiding the fate of the kingdom from behind closed doors.

The halls of the Magisterium were an architectural wonder in their own right. The walls of the building seemed to shift and shimmer like the surface of a deep lake, constantly changing as if they were alive. The floors, too, were alive with magic, and the very stones beneath one's feet seemed to hum with otherworldly energy. Within these halls, the most brilliant minds in Reldad gathered to study, debate, and explore the deepest mysteries of the magical arts. It was here that new spells were born, here that ancient secrets were uncovered, and here that the very boundaries of magic were pushed to their limits. To be accepted into the Magisterium was the highest honour a sorcerer could receive, but it was also a burden, for the power and responsibility of the magisters were immense, and their decisions could have far-reaching consequences for the entire kingdom.

Yet, for all its beauty, power, and intellectual wealth, Aetherion was not the only force shaping the fate of Reldad. Beyond its gleaming spires and the protective wards that surrounded it, the land itself—untamed and primal—whispered its secrets to those who would listen. To the south of Aetherion, the Verdant Wilds stretched out in an endless sea of green, a place where nature and magic coexisted in their purest forms. The Wilds were a world unto themselves, a realm of thick, ancient forests teeming with life and magic in equal measure. Here, the trees grew taller than the tallest towers of Aetherion, their trunks so thick that it would take a dozen men to encircle them with their arms. The canopies of these trees were so dense that sunlight barely touched the forest floor, and a deep, ethereal twilight prevailed even at midday.

The rivers that wound their way through the Wilds were unlike any other in Reldad. Their waters shimmered with an inner light, as though they were imbued with the magic of the land itself. It was said that the waters of the rivers could heal the sick, restore the lost, and even grant visions of the past and future. The very air in the Wilds was thick with enchantment, and those who ventured into the heart of the forests often found themselves touched by the magic that flowed freely through the land. It was in these forests that the elves, gnomes, and fae made their homes, living in perfect harmony with the land and weaving their lives—and their magic—into the natural order.

In the end, Aetherion and the Verdant Wilds, though vastly different in their form and function, were two sides of the same coin. One represented the heights of civilisation, the pursuit of knowledge, and the mastery of magic, while the other was a wild, untamed reflection of nature itself. Together, they defined the very essence of Reldad—a land where magic was not just a tool, but a living, breathing force that shaped every aspect of life.

The Kingdom's People

The people of Reldad were as diverse and varied as the land they inhabited, each race and culture carving out their place within the expansive kingdom. From the bustling cities built by humans to the hidden sanctuaries woven by the fae, the people of Reldad each brought something unique to the kingdom's rich tapestry. Their stories were intertwined with the land's magic, for the very essence of Reldad was shaped by the lives of its inhabitants. The kingdom, with its wide-reaching plains, towering mountains, deep forests, and glimmering seas, was home to those who wielded magic, knowledge, and the power of creation itself.

The most populous and visible of Reldad's inhabitants were the humans, whose cities and kingdoms spanned across the plains, valleys, and coasts of the realm. Human ambition was as vast as their numbers, and their capacity for creation and destruction was unmatched. In the sprawling plains of

Ydrath, human civilisation had risen to great heights. Towering fortresses stood on hilltops, offering both defence and a statement of their power, while bustling marketplaces thrived in the fertile heartlands. In the shadow of these fortresses, humans built their lives and their legacies, their ingenuity matched only by their unyielding drive to conquer challenges and improve their world. Despite their comparatively short lifespans, which seldom exceeded a century, the humans' hunger for knowledge and discovery had left an indelible mark on the land. It was said that where humans went, they transformed the land, shaping it through their architecture, agriculture, and innovation. From the forging of steel to the casting of intricate spells, humans had become the heart of Reldad's kingdoms.

In the south, beyond the human cities, lay the Verdant Wilds—a vast and ancient forest, home to creatures and races whose connection to the land was far deeper than that of any human. The fae, elusive and enchanting, had crafted their homes here, carving out sanctuaries within the heart of the enchanted forest. Their dwellings were not mere homes; they were works of living art, woven seamlessly into the very branches of ancient trees. The fae's cities were not built in the traditional sense, for they did not need walls or structures of stone and mortar. The forest itself provided for them, with trees as old as time offering shelter, and vines forming bridges between towering oaks. Their homes shimmered in the light, as though the forest had gifted them its essence to be used in their magical dwellings.

The fae possessed an innate connection to nature's magic, their existence entwined with the land in ways that no other race could replicate. Their songs—soft and ethereal—were carried on the wind and were said to possess healing properties. It was whispered that the fae could call the winds to calm the fiercest storms or coax the flowers to bloom in the dead of winter. Their magic was subtle, yet powerful, as natural as the tides or the passing of seasons. They understood the rhythms of the world in a way no other race could.

But while the fae lived in harmony with the wilderness, deep below the surface of Reldad's hills, the gnomes carved out their own domain—one of intellect, invention, and discovery. These small but brilliant beings were known for their remarkable ingenuity and technical expertise. Dwelling within the dark caverns beneath the hills, the gnomes had established subterranean cities that rivalled any aboveground settlement in complexity and design. They had an uncanny ability to blend magic with the natural energy of the earth. Geothermal vents provided the power to their workshops, where they crafted strange and wondrous machines—clockwork devices that seemed to run on both magic and the principles of engineering. Their creations were both awe-inspiring and practical, from intricate mechanical birds that flew on enchanted winds to alchemical brews that healed or poisoned with a single drop. To the people of Reldad, the gnomes were the kingdom's secret architects—rarely seen but always present in the quiet miracles of invention.

The gnomes' ingenuity extended beyond mere machines; they were pioneers in the field of magical alchemy, blending magic and science in ways that none other dared to attempt. Their inventions, powered by a deep understanding of the earth's natural forces, were often sought after by kings and rulers, who understood that the gnomes could unlock the mysteries of the world and push the boundaries of both magic and technology. The gnomes were not driven by ambition or conquest, but rather by an insatiable curiosity and a desire to understand the world's deepest workings.

Then, there were the elves—tall, ethereal beings whose connection to Reldad was as ancient as the land itself. The elves were a deeply spiritual people, their existence woven into the very fabric of the earth's magic. Their longevity far surpassed that of humans, with some elves having lived for millennia, and their wisdom was matched only by their mysterious nature. The elves had lived in harmony with Reldad's forests, rivers, and mountains for as long as any could remember, their lives intimately connected to the land and its creatures. Their presence was not always visible, for they moved through the world with an elusive grace, often hidden from mortal eyes, yet they were the stewards of the land. Their cities were hidden from outsiders, nestled deep within the heart of ancient forests or high in the mountaintops, where they had built their homes in perfect harmony with nature. The elven homes were often made of living wood, shaped by magic to grow into homes and spires that blended seamlessly with the landscape. They did not dominate the land, as humans often did, but instead worked alongside it, drawing power from its very essence.

The elves possessed a magic unlike any other. It was a magic that flowed through the rivers and the winds, a force that seemed to pulse with the heartbeat of the world itself. Their spells were subtle, woven into the very fabric of nature, and their connection to the land allowed them to communicate with the creatures of the forest, control the weather, and even shape the elements. Elven magic was not about domination but about understanding and balance. The elves were a peaceful people, but they would not hesitate to defend the land they held so dear if it were threatened. Their wisdom and compassion made them trusted allies, though their aloofness and otherworldly nature sometimes led others to misunderstand them. To outsiders, the elves often seemed unreadable, their faces blank with thought and their motives inscrutable. But those who earned their trust found that the elves were among the most empathetic beings in Reldad, guided by a profound love for the land and a deep understanding of its secrets.

Though the people of Reldad were separated by race, culture, and belief, they were united by the magic that flowed through their veins. This magic, a force both ancient and mysterious, was the true bond that connected all the peoples of the kingdom. It was a bond that transcended differences and could unite the races in times of peace—or tear them apart in times of conflict. Magic was not just a tool for the people of Reldad; it was a way of life, a force that shaped their destinies and connected them all to the land. Yet, despite the unity brought by magic, the people's differences were often a source of tension, and the kingdom was no stranger to conflict. Wars were fought over territories, resources, and the control of magic itself, as each race sought to preserve its own vision of Reldad's future.

But there were those who believed in the unity of the people, and their voices called for peace and understanding between the races. In times of crisis, when the very survival of Reldad hung in the balance, it was these voices that would be heard the loudest—reminding all the people of Reldad that, despite their differences, they shared a common bond that could never be broken: the magic that flowed through them all, the magic that made them who they were.

A World of Magic

Magic in Reldad was not just a part of life; it was the very essence of existence itself. It flowed through every leaf on every tree, every gust of wind, every crack of thunder, and every flicker of the stars above. To the people of Reldad, magic was as vital as air, water, or sunlight. It was not something to be learned alone in dusty books or locked away in vaults; it was alive, breathing, and ever-present. It surrounded the people in every moment, a force as natural and inevitable as the changing of seasons. To wield magic in Reldad was to touch the heart of the world, to commune with the elements themselves, and to become part of the very fabric of life.

From the humblest farmer to the mightiest sorcerer, magic was present in every corner of life. It was the foundation upon which society was built, and its influence reached across all aspects of existence. The farmer, standing beneath the great sky, would whisper an incantation as the earth beneath him shifted, coaxing the seeds he planted to grow into bountiful crops. The smith, hammer in hand, would call upon the fire to temper the steel, giving his weapons an edge sharper than the fiercest beast's claw. Magic was present in the every day, and it was both a tool and a gift that allowed life in Reldad to thrive.

However, while magic might have been common, its study and mastery were not. The schools of magic that flourished across the kingdom were numerous and varied, each rooted in the natural forces that governed the world. The most prevalent and widely practised was elemental magic. Earth, fire, water, and air—the basic elements that formed the world—were the foundation of magic as most knew it. This school of magic was ubiquitous, practised by everyone from the lowliest craftsman to the most powerful warlock. The connection between the elements and magic was so intrinsic to life in Reldad that the people of every village, town, and city used elemental spells in their daily lives.

The weavers of fire were among the most revered, for they could forge weapons of exceptional strength and durability. The fire element could be harnessed to temper metal, turning it into blades sharp enough to slice through the toughest hides or armour. These fire mages were often sought after by blacksmiths and soldiers, their skills indispensable in the crafting of tools and weapons. A single flick of the wrist, a quick word of incantation, and the fire would dance to their will, shaping the metal with an artful precision that was unparalleled. Fire, too, had other uses; it could heal wounds, purify water, or even serve as a means of transportation in the form of firestorms and fireball spells. Yet, as with all magic, it was a power that had to be controlled, for the fire that could create could also destroy.

The shapers of water were perhaps the most beloved in Reldad, for their magic could summon rain to end droughts, cleanse polluted rivers, and bring life to the earth in times of famine. Water had an ethereal, fluid quality that allowed it to flow with ease, adapting to the needs of the caster. In times of hardship, when the land grew dry and crops withered, the call of the water mages was the most welcomed. Their songs could coax clouds to gather and release their precious rain, bringing the blessings of water to parched soil. Their magic also had other, more subtle uses: restoring health to the sick, soothing wounds, and cooling fevered brows. For those who understood its depths, water could even be used to manipulate the tides, shape ice, or purify the air.

The air was another realm of magic, harnessed by those who could communicate with the winds. The air mages, often called 'wind whisperers,' could summon breezes to carry messages, conjure storms to clear the skies, or calm tempests at sea. They could move with the wind, travelling from place to place without the need for traditional means of transport. The wind, with its swift and unpredictable nature, was a fickle ally, and only those who understood the delicate balance of air could wield it with any degree of success. Masters of air could even turn invisible, their forms as fluid and fleeting as the wind itself. For the people of Reldad, air magic was often used in both battle and diplomacy, with the wind delivering messages across great distances or sweeping away enemies in a sudden, tempestuous fury.

But while elemental magic was the most common, there existed more rare and dangerous schools of magic, each with its own set of powers and dangers. Perhaps the most feared of these was empathis—the magic of emotion. To wield empathis was to understand and manipulate the innermost feelings of others. It was an incredibly powerful magic, but it came at a terrible cost. To control another's emotions was to risk losing oneself in the process. A person who wielded this magic had to maintain absolute control over their own heart, for any emotional imbalance could cause the magic to backfire. Those who could influence the sorrow, joy, fear, or rage of others were often seen with suspicion and distrust, for the power to manipulate a person's innermost thoughts and desires was dangerous. And even those who could wield it with purity of heart often struggled with the temptation to use their powers for less noble purposes.

Despite its rarity and the risks associated with it, Empathis was a sought-after skill, especially by those in positions of power. Kings and queens, generals and merchants, all sought out those who could help sway the hearts of their subjects. Empathis was not just a tool for persuasion; it was a weapon in the courts and battlefields of Reldad, capable of altering the course of wars or entire kingdoms. But such power was a double-edged sword. Those who could bend the hearts of others could also break them, and many who had sought this magic were lost to it, consumed by their own desires for control.

Then there was arcane magic, the most ancient and mysterious form of magic in Reldad. It was said to be the magic of the gods themselves, older than the world, and it held the power to reshape reality. Arcane magic was practised only by the most powerful and learned sorcerers, those who sought to unlock the deepest secrets of the universe. Masters of Arcane magic could bend time and space, manipulate the fabric of reality, and even challenge death itself.

But with such power comes great risk. The cost of failure was catastrophic, for arcane magic was unpredictable. A sorcerer who failed to control its raw energy could find themselves trapped in an endless loop of time, their body twisted into a form not their own, or their very soul torn apart and scattered across the realms. To practice arcane magic was to walk a razor-thin line between genius and madness. Those who succeeded were often revered as living gods, while those who failed were often forgotten, their names erased from history.

Yet, while magic was the most prominent force shaping life in Reldad, it was not the only one. Beneath the beauty of the kingdom, ancient and malevolent forces stirred, forces older than the gods themselves. These dark powers whispered in the shadows, waiting for the right moment to reveal themselves. Their magic was not elemental or arcane; it was primal, born of corruption and decay, a force that could tear apart the very fabric of reality. It was said that these ancient evils had once been banished to the corners of the world, sealed away by the gods themselves. But the seals were weakening, and the whispers of their return were growing louder. Magic, for all its beauty and power, was a double-edged sword. The very forces that brought life and prosperity could also bring destruction, and the people of Reldad knew that the balance of the world could shift in an instant, turning creation into ruin.

The Shadows Beneath the Earth

In the Western Marshes, where the light seldom touched, the Blackwater Marshes bred more than foul swamps and poisonous creatures. It was a land where the air itself seemed thick with unease, and the thick, misty fogs that rolled in from the distant sea were not only a sign of the land's foreboding nature but also a reminder of the terrible secrets it kept hidden beneath its stagnant waters. The marshes, a vast network of murky pools, treacherous quicksand, and twisting gnarled trees, were a place where few dared to wander, and fewer still ever returned from. They were the very embodiment of isolation, both physical and magical, where time itself seemed to slow and warp, like the sluggish current of the rivers that crawled through the swamps.

For centuries, the Blackwater Marshes had been avoided by the people of Reldad, a land full of rich lore and dark history. Travellers spoke of the region in hushed tones, their voices filled with fear and reverence. Among the stories, none were more persistent than the tales of ancient sorcery that had once lived and breathed within the heart of the marsh. It was said that long ago, a powerful order of sorcerers, known as the Obsidian Circle, had sought to bend the very forces of nature to their will. These dark practitioners had delved into forbidden magics, reaching deep into the earth and the elements, searching for ways to control not only the land but the fabric of reality itself. The Obsidian Circle had believed that by mastering the forces of both light and shadow, they could rule over all of Reldad and beyond.

At the height of their power, the circle had built great spires of stone that pierced the heavens, reaching towards the stars, while their magic resonated through the land like the beating of a dark heart. The very soil beneath their feet had been enchanted to obey their will, the rivers had flowed in patterns of their choosing, and the winds had carried their whispers. But with such power came great arrogance, and the circle's greed had driven them to attempt the ultimate act of magic—an act that would allow them to transcend mortality itself. In their hubris, they tried to bind the life force of Reldad itself, seeking to merge their essences with the land and the magic it held.

Their ritual was a terrible failure, one that shattered the very fabric of the land and left a scar on the marshes that could still be felt to this day. The great towers of the Obsidian Circle crumbled, their once-glorious spires now nothing more than ruins sunk deep into the earth. The sorcerers were consumed by their own power, their souls twisted and distorted by the magic they had unleashed. It was said that the land had rejected them, and in doing so, it had condemned them to an eternity of torment. The Blackwater Marshes became a place of death and despair, haunted by the souls of the fallen sorcerers, who still roamed the shadows, seeking to reclaim the power they had lost. And while the Obsidian Circle itself had been destroyed, the dark magic they had left behind lingered, dormant but not forgotten.

For centuries, the marshes had remained a place of myth and superstition, feared by all but the most desperate or foolish adventurers. Yet, there were whispers in the air, carried by the winds that swept across the land, that the magic of the circle had not died with them. Some believed it was still hidden deep beneath the waterlogged ground, waiting for the right moment to awaken, to resurface and claim the world once again. Those who had ventured into the marshes seeking answers never returned, and their fates became part of the growing legends that surrounded the cursed land. The world outside had forgotten the Blackwater Marshes, but the forces that lay dormant within it had not forgotten the world.

The Heart of Darkness: The Reldadan Mountains

Far to the east, where the land gave way to the jagged peaks of the Reldadan Mountains, another dark secret had festered for millennia. These mountains, towering and forbidding, seemed to pierce the very heavens, their snow-capped peaks lost in the clouds. The Reldadan range and its inhospitable terrain had kept most of Reldad's people from venturing too far into its depths. It was a place where even the most seasoned explorers turned back in fear, for the mountains were said to be riddled with hidden caves, narrow passes, and treacherous cliffs, many of which had never been fully mapped.

But it was not the perilous geography that made the Reldadan Mountains infamous. No, the mountains held a far darker secret—one that had remained hidden for centuries, buried in the forgotten corners of the world. Deep within the heart of the mountains, far beyond the reach of mortal hands, lay the remains of Raxis, an ancient sorcerer whose name was spoken only in whispers. Raxis was believed to have once been one of the greatest and most feared practitioners of arcane magic in all of Reldad. His power had been immense, his knowledge of the arcane arts vast and unparalleled. Legends spoke of Raxis's ability to manipulate time itself, to call upon forces beyond comprehension, and to command the very elements with a mere thought.

It was said that the few who had ventured into the mountains in search of Raxis had never returned, their bodies never found, their fates sealed by the sorcerer's dark magic. The land had become a place of mystery and foreboding, a place where the very rocks and stones whispered of ancient, forgotten power. Many had abandoned the search for Raxis, but there were still those who believed that the ancient sorcerer would one day return, bringing with him a storm of magic that could either save or destroy Reldad. No one knew for sure, but the possibility of his return haunted the kingdom like a shadow, always just out of reach, yet ever-present.

The Rising Threat

As time passed, the legends of the Blackwater Marshes and the Reldadan Mountains became little more than tales told around campfires, the dark histories of Reldad fading into myth. Yet there were still those who believed the ancient forces of evil slumbered beneath the earth, waiting for their moment to rise again. In the quiet corners of the kingdom, those who had studied the old texts and the forgotten prophecies knew that the time of awakening was near. The ancient sorceries, once thought to be lost to time, were stirring once again.

Across Reldad, strange occurrences had begun to unsettle the people: crops failing for no reason, animals acting strangely, and the air itself feeling thick with an unnatural tension. Whispers had begun to spread through the land, warnings of something ancient, something dark, stirring in the shadows. The time for these forgotten evils to rise again might be at hand. The fate of Reldad would soon be tested, as the shadows beneath the earth sought to reclaim the world they had once lost. Whether the kingdom would be able to withstand the storm, or whether it would fall to the very forces it had long forgotten, was a question that hung in the air like a storm cloud, waiting to break.

The Heroes of Reldad

It is against the backdrop of magic, mystery, and impending darkness that our tale begins. In the kingdom of

Reldad, a land brimming with enchantment and danger, an ancient evil stirs beneath the earth, threatening to tear asunder the fragile peace that has held the realm together for centuries. The kingdom braces for a storm—not one born of wind and rain, but of shadow and fire, a tempest of magic that will shake the foundations of the land. It is in these tumultuous times, when all seems poised on the brink of ruin, that three heroes rise, each touched by the forces of Reldad itself, each destined to shape the future of their world.

Eryndal Bethkalen: The Heart of Empathy

Eryndal Bethkalen was a young man marked by a rare and dangerous gift: the magic of empathis. Unlike the elemental forces of fire, water, earth, or air, Empathis allowed its wielders to feel and manipulate the emotions of others. To many, this ability was both a blessing and a curse—one that could heal or harm, depending on the wielder's intentions. For Eryndal, it had always been a burden, a constant presence in his life, one that he struggled to control. He had learned from an early age that his powers were not something to be wielded lightly; they were a force that could either bring about great peace or sow terrible chaos. The emotions of others were always within reach for Eryndal—like waves crashing relentlessly against a fragile shore.

Growing up in the city of Ilya, nestled in the plains of Ydrath, Eryndal had been taught from childhood to hide his gift. To show empathy for others in a world so filled with fear and greed was considered dangerous, and so he kept his heart guarded. He learned to disguise his emotions, to wear a mask in public, as he walked among the people of the kingdom. It wasn't until he encountered the devastating consequences of unchecked magical power that he realised the true nature of his gift.

Eryndal had witnessed firsthand the destruction caused by reckless magic—by those who had tried to force the land into submission, to wield power over it without understanding the delicate balance that magic required. He had watched as entire villages were destroyed by the violent outbursts of untrained sorcerers, as the land itself seemed to reject their attempts to control it. This had fuelled his determination to use his abilities not for personal gain, but to heal the wounds that others had caused. And as the storm of darkness began to stir across Reldad, it became clear that Eryndal's empathy would be the kingdom's greatest weapon.

Unlike the more obvious and forceful magics, empathis allowed Eryndal to reach into the hearts of others, to feel their pain, their fear, their hope. He could calm the raging storm of emotions within a person or, in dire circumstances, incite their darkest desires. The power to influence hearts was subtle but profound. It could mend broken alliances, quell riots, and even turn the tide of war. Eryndal would soon learn, however, that his greatest strength—and his greatest vulnerability—was his deep connection to the emotions of others. The line between understanding and becoming consumed by the emotions of others was razor-thin, and only by mastering his gift could he hope to wield it without losing himself in the process.

Soren Daliath Redborn: The Fae of Charisma and Deceit

Soren Daliath Redborn was a fae of incredible beauty, grace, and cunning. Born in the heart of the Verdant Wilds, she had been raised among the elves, gnomes, and fae who had long protected the forests and their ancient magic. The fae were known for their ability to weave charm into every word and every movement, their presence carrying an ethereal allure that could both enchant and manipulate those who crossed their path. Soren was no different. With eyes like the shimmering depths of the Sea of Sirrath and hair that seemed to sparkle like starlight, she possessed a magnetic pull that drew people to her—sometimes against their will.

But Soren's beauty was not her only weapon. Beneath her captivating exterior lay a mind sharp as a blade, a mind capable of reading people with unnerving accuracy. She could tell what others wanted before they even spoke it aloud, and with a smile or a soft word, she could convince them to act in her favour. In a kingdom so divided, where political intrigue and competing interests ran deep, Soren's talents were both a blessing and a curse. She was adept at weaving webs of influence, playing the great houses against one another, and securing the favour of kings and queens alike. Her power was not in brute force, but in subtle manipulation, the art of persuasion, and the skilful dance of diplomacy.

Despite her extraordinary abilities, Soren's heart was not entirely untouched by the darker aspects of her nature. Her charm, once used to bring unity and peace to the land, could also fracture alliances, sow discord, and manipulate others into playing roles in her grand schemes. She was capable of creating division as easily as she could forge unity, and it was a truth that weighed heavily on her soul. As the storm of darkness began to gather over Reldad, Soren knew that her gifts could either unite the kingdom's fractured forces in a time of need or divide them irrevocably, ensuring their fall. The choice would be hers to make, and in the balancing of power, she would have to decide how far she was willing to go to achieve her ends.

Roland Thorne Bardin: The Silent Strength of the Elven Warrior

Roland Thorne Bardin was the quietest of the three heroes, but his presence was no less powerful. A towering figure among the elves, Roland had spent most of his life honing his skills as a warrior, learning to move silently through the forests of Reldad, where even the faintest sound could mean the difference between life and death. Unlike his kin, who had long embraced the subtle arts of magic, Roland had chosen a path of martial discipline. He wielded the might of the earth itself, channelling the strength of the land into his sword and his fists. His power was one of unyielding force, not of magic or charm, but of pure determination and strength of will.

Roland's training had been rigorous, his mind sharpened by years of combat and survival in the harshest environments. He had been part of the elite elven rangers, tasked with protecting the borders of Reldad from external threats. The danger of the Wilds, of rogue sorcerers, and of otherworldly creatures, was ever-present in the northern territories, and Roland had learned to face these threats with the stoicism of a seasoned warrior. However, when the time came to confront a far greater threat—one that came not from the forests, but from the very bowels of the earth—Roland knew that his greatest challenge lay not in defeating an enemy with his blade, but in learning how to fight a force far darker and more insidious than any foe he had encountered before.

Though silent, Roland's strength was undeniable. When he fought, the earth itself seemed to tremble beneath his feet. He could channel the fury of the land into every strike, making his blows as unstoppable as a boulder crashing down from a mountain peak. His loyalty to his comrades was unwavering, and in their darkest moments, it was Roland's strength and quiet determination that would hold them together. While Eryndal could heal with empathy, and Soren could manipulate the minds of others, it was Roland who would stand as an immovable force against the darkness, a guardian whose loyalty to Reldad was beyond question.

A Kingdom's Last Hope

Together, these three heroes—Eryndal Bethkalen, Soren Daliath Redborn, and Roland Thorne Bardin—would face an enemy unlike any Reldad had ever known. The forces that sought to plunge the kingdom into darkness were ancient and terrible, and the odds were stacked against them. Yet, in the strength of their bond, in the diversity of their gifts, lay the last hope for the future of the kingdom. The tale of Reldad was about to be written in the fires of battle, in the whispers of magic, and in the hearts of its greatest champions. With their courage, their unity, and their willingness to face the shadows, they would determine whether Reldad would rise to meet its destiny or fall beneath the weight of its darkest fears.

Chapter 2
The Return of the Shadow

In the tranquil kingdom of Reldad, under a vast expanse of glittering stars, there was once a golden era when darkness was but a distant memory whispered only in forgotten tales. For centuries, the land flourished, its beauty unmatched and its harmony unbroken. From the fertile plains that stretched endlessly towards the horizon to the lush, ancient forests alive with the songs of nature, Reldad was a paradise. Its cities were jewels scattered across the landscape: **Anarith**, a vibrant coastal hub where trade and culture thrived, and **Glenstone**, a serene village nestled in the verdant embrace of the Mithran Valley, where time seemed to move more slowly, in rhythm with the natural world.

At the kingdom's edge, where the Varnor Mountains met the boundless expanse of the Bershian Sea, stood **Elderion Citadel**, a masterpiece of stone and magic. From its lofty halls, the kings and queens of Reldad ruled wisely, their wisdom preserved in the ancient tomes of the royal library. The castle itself seemed to glow with the light of prosperity, its spires reaching towards the heavens as if in communion with the gods. Here, magic thrived as naturally as the air itself, and the world seemed limitless, its potential as boundless as the imaginations of its people.

But even the brightest light casts shadows.

The Rise of Raxis

From beyond the **Veil of Seraphran**, a foreboding place spoken of in hushed tones, a shadow descended upon Reldad. It was unlike anything the kingdom had known—a force so consuming it seemed to drain the light from the sky and the hope from the hearts of all who beheld it. Its name was **Raxis**, a being of unfathomable darkness whose origins were shrouded in myth. Some whispered that he was born of cursed magic in the barren **Tivrah Desert**, where gods of old had fallen silent. Others claimed he had risen from the depths of the **Bershian Sea**, a monstrous echo of the abyss itself.

Raxis's Rise to Madness

Raxis had been no ordinary sorcerer. In his prime, he had stood as one of the most powerful magisters of the age, a master of arcane magic who could bend the very fabric of reality to his will. But his brilliance was matched only by his arrogance. When the Obsidian Circle crumbled under the weight of its members' collective greed and ambition, Raxis alone emerged unscathed. He saw their failure not as a warning but as an opportunity. The collapse of the circle left a vacuum of power, one that Raxis sought to fill by claiming the Crown of Eternity, a mythical artefact said to grant its wielder dominion over all magic in Reldad.

The Crown, forged in the dawn of time by the gods themselves, had been hidden for centuries, guarded by powerful wards and ancient seals. Raxis, however, was relentless. He unearthed the Crown in the Forsaken Plains, a desolate wasteland where the winds carried whispers of the past. But wielding the Crown was no simple feat—it demanded a soul unyielding and unbroken. Raxis believed himself worthy, and in his hubris, he attempted to bind the Crown's power to himself through a forbidden ritual. He sought to transcend mortality, to merge his essence with the magic of the land and become eternal.

But the ritual went horribly wrong. The Crown, unwilling to yield to his will, shattered in a burst of cataclysmic energy, tearing the very ground asunder. The explosion created a rift in the Forsaken Plains, a scar on the land that would never heal. Worse still, Raxis's soul was splintered, fragmented by the raw magic he had sought to command. Yet even in this broken state, Raxis was a force to be reckoned with. The Crown's fragmented power remained within him, twisting his mind and body into something monstrous.

Lord Thalion Bethkalen's Stand

Word of Raxis's ritual reached Lord Thalion Bethkalen in the Harden Fields, where he had been marshalling his forces against the growing threat of the sorcerer. Thalion, a man of unshakeable resolve and unparalleled skill in both warfare and magic, knew that Raxis could not be allowed to consolidate his newfound power. The fate of Reldad hung in the balance. Leading an alliance of humans, elves, fae and gnomes, Thalion marched to confront the sorcerer on the Forsaken Plains.

The battle began under a sky heavy with storms as if the heavens themselves recoiled from the carnage to come. Raxis's forces were an unholy amalgamation of his will: shadow-beasts summoned from the void, twisted constructs powered by magic, and mortal followers drawn to his promises of power and immortality. Against them stood Thalion's army, a coalition of Reldad's finest.

Magic collided with steel as the battle raged across the plains. The very earth trembled beneath the clash of forces, and the air crackled with arcane energy. Thalion, clad in enchanted armour and wielding the legendary blade Dawnsever, led his troops with unyielding determination. He cut through Raxis's minions like a force of nature, his presence rallying his warriors even in the face of overwhelming odds.

The Final Confrontation

The turning point came when Thalion and his elite guard pushed through the heart of Raxis's forces, confronting the sorcerer himself. Raxis, a figure wreathed in darkness and arcane fire, was no longer entirely human. His fragmented soul and the shattered power of the Crown had transformed him into something otherworldly. His voice, echoing with a thousand whispers, promised destruction to all who defied him.

The duel between Thalion and Raxis was a spectacle of power and fury. Raxis unleashed torrents of raw magic, bending the elements to his will and summoning storms of fire and ice to annihilate his foe. But Thalion was not easily broken. Guided by his indomitable will and a profound connection to the land's magic, he parried Raxis's assaults, his blade glowing with a light that seemed to cut through the very darkness that surrounded the sorcerer.

The clash lasted for what felt like hours, each strike shaking the earth and sending shockwaves across the battlefield. Thalion's forces, inspired by their leader's bravery, pushed back against Raxis's minions, turning the tide of the battle. But even as victory seemed within reach, Raxis unleashed a final, desperate attack—a surge of chaotic energy that threatened to obliterate both armies and the land itself.

The Sacrifice

In that moment, Thalion made a choice. Drawing upon every ounce of his strength and magic, he channelled the power of the land into Dawnsever, forging a single, devastating strike. The blade pierced Raxis's chest, and with it, the fractured remnants of the Crown's power. The resulting explosion was blinding, a wave of light and sound that tore through the battlefield.

When the dust settled, Raxis was gone. His physical form had been obliterated, his fragmented soul cast into the void between time and space. The Crown of Eternity, too, was no more, its shards scattered across the Forsaken Plains. Thalion stood amidst the wreckage, his armour battered, his body broken—but victorious. The battle was won, but at great cost.

The Legacy of the Broken Crown

The Forsaken Plains, already a desolate place, became a haunted land, its scars a testament to the devastation wrought by Raxis's ambition. The rift created by the ritual remained, a gaping wound in the fabric of reality that pulsed with unstable magic. Scholars and adventurers who ventured too close often reported hearing whispers—echoes of Raxis's voice, promising vengeance.

Thalion returned to the Harden Fields a hero, but he bore the weight of his victory heavily. The destruction he had witnessed, the lives lost in the battle, and the lingering threat of Raxis's possible return haunted him for the rest of his days. The name of Raxis, once a symbol of power and brilliance, became a cautionary tale, a reminder of the dangers of unchecked ambition and the price of hubris.

As for Raxis, his fate remained a mystery. Some believed that the void had consumed him entirely, erasing his existence from time itself. Others whispered that fragments of his soul lingered, reaching out from the rift, waiting for an opportunity to return. The winds that howled through the Reldadan Mountains carried an eerie note as if the land itself mourned—or feared—his potential resurgence.

Thus, the Battle of the Broken Crown became a pivotal chapter in Reldad's history, a story of heroism and sacrifice, of the enduring strength of those who fight for the greater good, and of the ever-present shadow of those who would seek to destroy it.

Whispers of a Return

Though Raxis's reign of terror had ended, his shadow refused to be forgotten. Like a ghost clinging to the edges of memory, the spectre of his name hovered over Reldad. Stories of his defeat, often recounted by elders around flickering hearth fires, served as both a warning and a lingering question: Was he truly gone? The fall of Raxis in the Battle of the Broken Crown had shattered more than just the land—it had shaken the kingdom's understanding of what magic could do and the price it exacted. Yet, despite the certainty with which Lord Thalion Bethkalen had struck down the sorcerer, whispers persisted.

These whispers wove through every corner of the kingdom, from its sunlit plains to its shadowed depths. They crept into the Tivrah Desert, where the vast, golden sands stretched endlessly, shimmering under an unforgiving sun. Once a place of mystery, the desert had become a land of dread. Travellers who dared to traverse its rolling dunes reported eerie phenomena: strange, dark shapes flickering on the horizon, never drawing closer yet never fading away; voices that rode on the desert wind, too soft to comprehend yet too chilling to ignore. Some spoke of ruins newly uncovered by shifting sands—structures bearing carvings that depicted ancient sorcery and symbols eerily reminiscent of Raxis's rise to power.

A Sea Stirred by Secrets

In the Bershian Sea to the east, the unease took on a different form. The waters, once pristine and full of life, had become a place of foreboding. Sailors swore they saw lights glimmering beneath the waves—unearthly hues of blue and green that moved with an unnatural grace. Some claimed the lights were the remnants of lost civilisations, drawn up by the echoes of Raxis's magic.

Others believed the sorcerer himself stirred in the sea's depths, his fragmented soul reaching out from its timeless void. More than one ship failed to return from its voyage, swallowed by storms that appeared without warning or by waters that suddenly turned still and dark, as though holding their breath.

Fishermen spoke of nets coming back empty, or worse, tangled with things they could not explain—seaweed that glowed faintly in the dark, bones of creatures no one could identify, and once, an object that resembled a piece of broken obsidian, etched with lines that seemed to pulse faintly under the moonlight. The Bershian Sea had always carried an air of mystery, but now it had become a harbinger of unease, its depths an unknown frontier that many feared to test.

Signs in the Heartland

Even in the heart of Reldad, where life had begun to return to normal, a creeping unease settled over the land. Glenstone, known for its golden fields and tranquil meadows, was the breadbasket of the kingdom, a place where life should have been simple and serene. Yet, on certain nights, a cold wind would sweep through the fields, carrying with it a chill that seemed unnatural for the season. Farmers reported finding their crops wilting overnight, as though touched by an unseen blight. Children, playing in the fields, sometimes paused mid-laughter, staring at shadows that should not have moved.

In the town square, statues that had stood for centuries began to change. Cracks appeared along their surfaces, not from age or weather, but from something else. Observant townsfolk swore the faces of the statues shifted when no one was looking—an impossible, horrifying transformation that left the stone figures appearing more malevolent, their leering gazes following passersby. Priests were called to bless the town, but their prayers did little to quell the growing fear.

To the west, in the Mithran Valley, the forests seemed to breathe with unease. Once a haven of peace and natural beauty, the valley was a place of thick woods, shimmering streams, and life in abundance. But the animals that roamed these woods began to behave strangely. Deer froze at the sound of whispers carried by the wind. Wolves, normally elusive and wary of humans, circled the edges of settlements, their golden eyes glowing with an unnatural intensity. Birds, once filling the forest with their songs, grew silent, their absence leaving an unsettling void. Hunters who ventured deep into the forest spoke of feeling watched, their every step echoing too loudly in the unnatural stillness.

Rebuilding in the Shadow of War

Despite these troubling signs, the people of Reldad worked tirelessly to rebuild what the Great War had taken from them. Cities razed by Raxis's minions were reconstructed, their walls made higher and their defences stronger. Villages burned to ash rose again, with homes sturdier than before. Fields destroyed by battles were tilled anew, their soil enriched with the sweat and determination of survivors. Yet even in the midst of renewal, the scars of the past lingered.

The elders who had lived through the war could not forget the fear that had gripped them. For every stone laid in the name of peace, there was a whispered prayer that it would not crumble under the weight of a future conflict. Families mourned those lost to the horrors of Raxis's reign, their memories honoured in quiet ceremonies and through the planting of trees—each sapling a symbol of hope that life might continue despite the darkness.

However, the unease gnawed at the edges of their peace. Those who had fought in the war, warriors and mages alike, spoke in hushed tones of the unnatural quiet that often followed them. Veterans of the Battle of the Broken Crown described dreams that haunted them, visions of Raxis's fragmented form whispering promises of power and vengeance. He was not simply a memory to them—he was a presence, lurking on the edges of their consciousness.

Scholars and Seekers

The whispers of Raxis's potential return did not go unnoticed by the kingdom's scholars and mages. In the grand halls of Aetherion, the magisters debated fiercely over the signs. Some dismissed them as the natural aftershocks of a magical cataclysm as great as Raxis's fall. Magic, they argued, was like a river; when disrupted, it would take time to settle back into its course. But others were not so sure. The rift created by Raxis's failed ritual still pulsed faintly in the Forsaken Plains, a gaping wound in the world that resisted all efforts to close it.

Magisters tasked with studying the rift reported disturbing findings: anomalies in the flow of magic, strange echoes that seemed to emanate from the void, and, most troubling of all, the sensation of being watched when they stood too close. One particularly daring scholar, a fae named Kaelith Serin, claimed to have seen a figure moving within the rift—a shadowy silhouette that bore an eerie resemblance to Raxis himself. Her testimony, though dismissed by many as hysteria, sent ripples of fear through the Magisterium.

Beyond Aetherion, adventurers and treasure hunters began to scour the land, seeking fragments of the Crown of Eternity. Though its pieces had been scattered after the Battle of the Broken Crown, rumours persisted that they still held fragments of their original power. The prospect of such power drew many, both noble and corrupt, to the Forsaken Plains. Few returned, and those who did speak of horrors lurking in the desolation—twisted creatures, unnatural storms, and voices that seemed to mock them from the shadows.

The Unspoken Truth

Beneath all the speculation and fear lay a truth that few dared to voice: Raxis's shadow was not merely a memory, but a warning. The signs of his influence—if they were indeed his—suggested that he had not been destroyed, but merely displaced. Perhaps his fractured soul still lingered, caught in the void between worlds, waiting for an opportunity to return. Or perhaps his essence had seeped into the very fabric of Reldad, corrupting it from within.

The kingdom's peace was a fragile thing, its foundation trembling under the weight of this unspoken truth. As life continued and the people tried to move on, the shadow of Raxis remained—a reminder that the battle for Reldad's future was far from over. The land itself seemed to sense it, its magic fluctuating unpredictably, its creatures growing restless, its people haunted by whispers of darkness they could not escape.

And so, Reldad braced itself for what was to come. For though Raxis had fallen, his story was not yet finished. The whispers carried on the wind, the lights beneath the sea, the shadows that danced across the desert sands—they all pointed to one inevitable conclusion: the darkness was stirring once more, and Reldad would need its heroes again.

A Kingdom in Waiting

Reldad was a land of contrasts—lush fields that met jagged mountains, ancient forests that bordered sprawling cities, and tranquil waters that carried the weight of untold mysteries. Yet, for all its beauty, a sense of unease had begun to creep into the hearts of its people. Beyond its borders lay a wide and enigmatic world, a tapestry of wonders and dangers that no cartographer could fully capture, and no historian could entirely chronicle. These distant lands, with their own secrets and stories, seemed to press ever closer, as if the boundaries of Reldad were no longer enough to keep the unknown at bay.

The **Varnor Peaks**, rising high to the north, loomed as both a barrier and a mystery. These towering mountains were wreathed in perpetual mist, their craggy silhouettes etched against the sky like ancient sentinels. The peaks were more than a physical divide; they were the stuff of legend, their snow-capped summits whispered to conceal gateways to other realms. It was said that strange lights often danced atop the peaks during the darkest nights, and those daring—or foolish—enough to climb higher than the clouds sometimes disappeared, never to return. Few who lived near the base of the mountains doubted these stories, for the winds that howled down from the heights carried whispers in languages long forgotten, chilling even the bravest souls.

Beyond the Varnor Mountains lay the **Bershian Sea,** stretched vast and mysterious, its waters an endless expanse of shifting blue and grey. Sailors who ventured too far from Reldad's shores often returned with wild tales, their faces pale and their eyes hollow with terror—or else they did not return at all. It was said that beneath the waves lurked cities older than Reldad itself, their spires and domes glowing faintly in the depths. Strange lights often flickered across the sea's surface, casting eerie reflections that made even seasoned mariners hesitant to set sail. Rumours of great serpents and shadowy leviathans only added to the Bershian's mystique, making it a place of both wonder and fear. Still, there were those who braved its waters, drawn by dreams of reaching the distant, uncharted shores that lay beyond the horizon.

To the **west**, the once-picturesque **Mithran Valley** had grown shrouded in shadow. Once celebrated for its serene beauty—fields of golden wildflowers stretching as far as the eye could see, cradled by emerald forests—it was now a place of caution. A faint, oppressive fog seemed to cling to the valley, even on the brightest days, and the usual songs of birds and rustle of deer were eerily absent. Travellers whispered of shadows moving among the trees, their forms indistinct but unmistakably watching. The paths that had once been the safest in all of Reldad were now avoided by most, and even the bravest mercenaries thought twice before accepting contracts to pass through the valley. It was as if the land itself had grown wary, recoiling from some unseen presence.

Within Reldad's borders, the **people** tried to hold onto their lives, their routines, and their hope. Yet they were not blind to the signs of change. The magic that had long been their salvation—the same force that had kept their crops growing, their cities thriving, and their lands protected—had become unpredictable. Farmers noticed their charms to summon rain faltering, with sudden storms bringing destruction rather than sustenance. Artisans reported their enchanted tools sparking erratically, as though resisting their commands. Even the magisters, the kingdom's most learned and disciplined sorcerers, grew troubled as ancient wards flickered and faded, their enchantments unravelling without explanation.

Whispers began to spread across the kingdom, carried from one hearth fire to the next. These whispers were not of armies gathering on the horizon or kings warring for thrones but of something far more insidious—**unseen forces stirring in the dark**. In isolated villages, reports surfaced of strange occurrences: livestock vanishing overnight, wells running dry despite no drought, and entire groves of trees withering as though drained of life. At first, these accounts were dismissed as the fabrications of frightened peasants, but as the stories grew more frequent and more detailed, even the sceptics began to listen. The descriptions of shadowy figures, ethereal and silent, were too similar to ignore, and the chilling realisation began to dawn that something ancient and malevolent was waking.

In the quiet corners of the kingdom, where **forests met fields and mountains met seas**, the signs of change were becoming undeniable. Birds took flight in erratic patterns, their usual migratory routes altered as though they sensed something the people of Reldad could not. The animals of the wild grew restless, their movements marked by a strange urgency. The rivers, once steady and calm, now swirled with unnatural currents, their waters colder than they should have been. Even the earth itself seemed to tremble now and then, sending faint vibrations through the soles of those who worked the fields or travelled the roads.

Among the cities, a **growing unease** began to settle over the populace. In Glenstone, a prosperous town nestled amid golden fields, the sun seemed to dim ever so slightly at dusk, casting longer shadows than it should. In Mithrold, where the towering spires of the Magisters' Hall pierced the heavens, the apprentices reported hearing faint, disembodied voices echoing through the stone corridors at night. And in Aetherion, the floating city that was the heart of Reldad's magic, a strange crack had appeared in one of the ancient crystal pylons that anchored the city to the sky. Though the magisters assured the people that the crack was of no concern, the faint hum that now emanated from it spoke otherwise.

At the edges of these happenings, a name began to resurface in hushed tones: **Raxis**. Once a nightmare long buried in the annals of history, the name now carried a weight that caused even the boldest to fall silent. Could it be that the ancient sorcerer, cast down in the Battle of the Broken Crown, was stirring once more? The elders, who had lived long enough to remember the stories of his reign, exchanged wary glances as they recounted the old tales. Raxis's fall had not been clean or absolute. His body had been consumed, but his essence—his power—was said to have been scattered, hidden in the darkest recesses of the world. If he were to return, it would not be as the man he once was but as something far more terrible.

For the people of Reldad, the question was no longer whether peace could last forever—it was whether it could last another year. The world felt as though it stood on a precipice, teetering between the fragile present and an uncertain future. And as the **stars turned overhead**, their light faint against the growing darkness, the winds carried whispers of what was to come.

In the distant corners of the world, where **ancient powers stirred** in shadowed recesses, the final question of Raxis's fate was answered in silence. He had not been destroyed. He had waited, patient and unyielding, gathering strength in the cracks of time and the folds of forgotten realms. His return was no longer a question of *if*—it was a question of *when*. Already, his influence was seeping through the boundaries of the world, bending the magic of Reldad to his will.

As **farmers worked their fields**, their ploughs turned up more than the soil. Artefacts—stone fragments etched with glowing runes—appeared in the earth, pulsing faintly with an ancient energy. The magisters, upon examining these objects, could only offer uneasy conclusions: they were not of this age, nor of any age recorded in their tomes. These were remnants of something older than Reldad itself, something tied to the primal forces of the world. What troubled them most was the sensation each object exuded, a faint but unmistakable aura of hunger, as though they were reaching out for something—or someone.

The **tides of magic**, once steady and predictable, now surged with erratic force. The elements seemed to rebel against their users, refusing to be commended as they had been for centuries. The fire burned hotter and wilder; water froze where it should have flowed, and the winds whispered secrets that no ear could decipher. These disturbances were no accident; they were warnings. The balance of the world was shifting, its equilibrium unravelling under the strain of a power too great to remain dormant.

The **people of Reldad**, from the highest towers of Aetherion to the humblest farms of the Verdant Wilds, could sense the change in the air. Children woke from nightmares, their screams echoing with words they could not remember but that left their parents shaken. Travellers found themselves avoiding certain roads and paths, feeling an inexplicable dread as they approached. Even the most hardened warriors felt unease, their hands gripping hilts tighter as if anticipating a foe that had not yet revealed itself.

And as the kingdom stood on the **cusp of a new era**, the horizon seemed to darken with each passing day. The **shadow of Raxis** was no longer a memory; it was a presence, faint but undeniable, creeping into the hearts of the land. The people of Reldad looked to their leaders, their heroes, and their scholars for guidance. Yet even the wisest among them could offer only one truth: the kingdom's fate would not be decided by the past but by those who dared to face the looming storm.

The **winds carried whispers**, and the whispers carried a warning: the world was no longer waiting for Raxis. He was already here.

Chapter 3
The Return of Raxis

For years, the name **Raxis** lingered in the shadows of memory, spoken only in whispers—a nightmare consigned to history. The Dark Lord, whose reign of terror had once plunged Reldad into chaos, was believed destroyed in a final, desperate battle. His armies scattered, his body obliterated, and his dominion over the land seemingly broken. Yet as generations passed, the certainty of his death began to waver. Shadows crept back into the edges of the kingdom and whispers of dread carried on the winds.

The return began as a subtle hum beneath the surface of Reldad, an unease that the land itself seemed to feel. The vibrant fields dulled, animals grew skittish, and the air turned unnaturally still. What started as faint disturbances soon grew into unmistakable signs—events that no longer allowed the people to deny the truth.

The First Signs

It began subtly, almost innocuously. In the remote villages of the Mithran Valley, where thick mist clung to the ground and the sun's light seemed perpetually dimmed, farmers spoke of fleeting shadows. At first, it was just a figure or two—vague and shapeless, lingering at the edge of their fields as dusk fell. Some thought it a trick of the light, the interplay of shadow and fog. Others blamed restless spirits or wayward travellers.

But soon, these figures became more distinct. They moved with unnatural speed and precision, their shapes too fluid to be human yet too corporeal to be ghosts. When one farmer claimed to see red eyes glowing in the darkness, his story was dismissed with laughter. Yet, when entire families began refusing to leave their homes after sunset, the laughter turned to unease.

In Anarith, the coastal city perched on the southern edge of the Bershian Sea, the fishermen spoke of shadows beneath the waves. At first, it was subtle: dark shapes flitting through the depths, too large to be mere fish. Then nets began coming up empty, slashed to ribbons as though something sharp and deliberate had torn through them. Boats moored near the shore were found adrift, their hulls splintered as if gnawed upon by unseen forces. The fishermen, usually pragmatic folk, began abandoning the waters entirely, their livelihoods sacrificed to an inexplicable fear.

Strangers also began to appear. They came hooded and cloaked, moving silently through towns and cities alike. They carried no wares and spoke to no one. Merchants noted their presence but quickly found their stalls avoided by these figures. Innkeepers recalled renting rooms only to find them empty the next morning, with not even a trace of their occupants. These figures were ghosts in all but name, their purpose as unknowable as their identities.

The scattered rumours converged into a chilling pattern: **the world was being watched.**

The Murder of the Elders

The first undeniable act of darkness came with blood, and its ripples would reach every corner of Reldad.

The Death of Seraphis

In the heart of the mystical **Heartwood**, Seraphis, an elder of the faes, was found dead beneath the ancient boughs of the Mother Tree. Seraphis had been a symbol of wisdom and strength, his life spanning centuries. The runes carved into his flesh were unlike anything the faes had seen—ancient symbols that pulsed faintly with black magic. The trees themselves seemed to mourn his death, their leaves wilting as though life itself recoiled from the dark energy radiating from his body.

The faes, long protected by the ethereal wards of their homeland, were gripped by fear. It was an unthinkable violation—dark magic breaching their sacred borders. The whispers that had seemed distant now felt dangerously close. Among the fae council, debates erupted about strengthening their defences, but the truth was unavoidable: **Raxis's shadow had reached even their sanctuaries.**

The Warning in Yrdain

While the faes reeled from their loss, the elves faced their own tragedy in **Yrdain**, the ancient stronghold nestled within the forested peaks of the Eastern Mountains. Lord Aeloran, revered for his wisdom and diplomacy, was found dead in his private chamber. Above his lifeless body, burned into the stone, was the unmistakable sigil of Raxis: a serpent devouring its own tail.

The elves were a proud and vigilant people, their magic rivalled only by their cunning. For an assassin—or worse, dark magic—to breach the walls of Yrdain was inconceivable. Lord Aeloran's death was more than a blow to their leadership; it was a calculated strike at their confidence. For centuries, the elves had prided themselves on their impenetrable defences. Now, they realised their walls could be breached and their leaders targeted. Fear spread among their ranks, and whispers of betrayal crept into their once-unified halls.

Chaos Beneath the Earth

Deep beneath the surface, the **Gnome Kingdoms** faced a subtler but equally sinister threat. The tremors began as minor inconveniences—tools falling from shelves, precarious bridges swaying above cavernous drops. But over time, they grew stronger. Intricate tunnels carved with millennia of precision collapsed, crushing homes and workshops. The gnomes, known for their engineering prowess, scrambled to stabilise their subterranean world, but their efforts were thwarted by a darkness they could not name.

The death of **Garthil Ironfoot**, a beloved craftsman and innovator, came as a shock. His body was discovered in his workshop, surrounded by glowing sigils etched into the stone floor. These symbols, written in a language the gnomes could not decipher, radiated a faint hum that resonated through the tunnels like a warning bell. Garthil's death was not just a loss of life; it was an attack on the ingenuity and resilience that defined the gnome people. For the first time in centuries, they found themselves truly afraid.

The Fall of Lord Thalion

The final and most devastating blow came to the humans of Reldad. **Lord Thalion Bethkalen**, steadfast leader of the human council and the voice of reason in turbulent times, was found dead beneath the Grand Oak—a sacred tree that had stood at the heart of Reldad for generations. His throat had been cut with brutal precision, and the serpent sigil was branded into his chest, seared so deeply that the smell of burned flesh lingered in the air long after his body was discovered.

Lord Thalion had been more than a leader. He was a symbol of hope, a man who had stood against the darkness of Raxis during the Battle of the Broken Crown and had led Reldad into its golden age of peace. His death was not merely a murder; it was a declaration. It sent an unmistakable message to the people of Reldad: **Raxis's shadow was no longer confined to the past. It had returned to claim the present.**

Eryndal's Burden

With Thalion's death, the human council was left fractured and leaderless. All eyes turned to his son, **Eryndal Bethkalen**, who was just coming of age. Though untested and still grieving, Eryndal carried his father's bloodline—and with it, the expectations of an entire race.

At first, the council hesitated to recognise Eryndal's authority. He was young, barely a man by their standards, and had spent much of his youth studying his rare **empathis abilities** rather than learning the intricacies of governance. But as the murders continued and fear spread, the people clamoured for stability. They remembered Thalion's wisdom and strength and began to see those same qualities budding in Eryndal. His ability to sense and connect with the emotions of others—a skill inherited from his lineage—became a source of comfort to his people.

Still, the weight of leadership was immense. Eryndal found himself thrust into an arena of political manoeuvring, facing experienced council members who doubted his resolve. Yet, as weeks passed, he proved himself in small but meaningful ways. He listened to the fears of his people, mediated disputes within the council, and began working closely with the magisters to strengthen Reldad's defences.

Eryndal's youth, which had once been seen as a weakness, became his strength. His empathy allowed him to inspire hope in a kingdom on the brink of despair. Slowly but surely, he began to embody the legacy of his father, though he knew the shadow looming over Reldad was far greater than anything Thalion had faced.

A Kingdom in Fear

The murders did not occur in isolation. Each death sent shockwaves through its respective community, but together, they formed a pattern that no one could ignore. The fae, the elves, the gnomes, and the humans—all the great peoples of Reldad—had been struck. Their leaders had been targeted with precision, their deaths laced with symbolism and dark magic. The message was clear: **Raxis was not merely returning. He was already here, his presence bleeding into the fabric of their world.**

Fear took root in the hearts of the people. Villages fortified their borders, and cities placed curfews to keep their citizens indoors after dark. Merchants avoided travel, cutting off vital trade routes and plunging smaller towns into scarcity. Even the magisters, the most powerful wielders of magic in the land, found themselves at a loss. The dark magic that marked each murder defied their understanding, as though it came from a source beyond the laws of their world.

The natural world also began to reflect the growing darkness. Rivers that once flowed clear and steady now ran sluggish and murky, their waters colder than they should have been. Crops withered despite careful tending, and animals grew skittish, their behaviour erratic and aggressive. Even the winds carried an unease, their whispers hinting at something ancient and malevolent stirring just beyond the veil of the known world.

The Return of Raxis

As the weeks turned to months, the signs of Raxis's return became undeniable. His influence seeped into every corner of the kingdom, bending nature and magic to his will. The murders were only the beginning—a prelude to a much larger symphony of chaos and destruction.

Somewhere, in the shadowed recesses of the world, Raxis' soul stirred fully awake. His exile had been long, but it had not broken him. If anything, it had refined his purpose, sharpening his hatred for the realm that had cast him down. He would not return quietly. **He would return to claim everything.**

A Fateful Meeting

The loss of Lord Thalion Bethkalen had shaken the human race, but for his son, Eryndal, it was a deeply personal wound. Thrust into leadership far earlier than expected, the young warrior found himself standing in his father's shadow, both inspired and burdened by the weight of Thalion's legacy.

For years, Thalion had warned that Raxis's dark influence might one day reemerge, carried forward by loyal followers who had survived the Great War. Eryndal, like many of his generation, had dismissed such fears. To him, they were ghost stories, relics of a bygone era. But now, his father's lifeless body and the serpent sigil seared into his flesh were stark reminders that the darkness had not been defeated—it had merely waited for its time to strike.

Eryndal's grief threatened to consume him, but the demands of leadership gave him little time to mourn. As the days turned into weeks, the young leader threw himself into the task of investigating his father's murder, determined to find those responsible and stop the growing shadow spreading across Reldad.

The Gathering of the Four Races

Eryndal's search for answers soon led him to a clandestine meeting of the four races—humans, faes, elves, and gnomes. The gathering was held in secret deep within the ancient

Hollow of Accord, a place where representatives of the races had once forged an alliance against Raxis centuries before.

The Hollow was a natural amphitheatre surrounded by towering stone spires and shielded by a magical barrier that concealed its location. The air within the Hollow felt heavy with history, the weight of old oaths pressing down on all who entered. It was here that Eryndal met two others whose lives had been similarly scarred by the recent wave of tragedies.

Soren Daliath Redborn

The first was **Soren Daliath Redborn**, a fae emissary from the Heartwood. Soren's presence was commanding, her movements graceful yet deliberate, her voice carrying a quiet power that demanded attention. She was gifted with the rare and dangerous ability to sway minds—a talent that made her both a diplomat and a weapon.

Though she appeared serene, Soren's ethereal beauty belied a ferocious resolve. She had been chosen by the faes not only for her abilities but also for her relentless dedication to protecting her people. The death of Seraphis, a revered elder of the fae, had shaken the Heartwood to its core, and Soren had taken it upon herself to uncover the truth behind the murder.

As Soren spoke of her investigation, Eryndal noted the steel in her voice. "The wards of the Heartwood are failing," she said, her golden eyes narrowing.

"The magic that has protected my people for centuries is unravelling, and Seraphis's death was no accident. Whoever killed him knew our defences and sought to weaken them further. We cannot face this threat alone."

Roland Thorne Bardin

The second was **Roland Thorne Bardin**, an elven warrior who had served as the closest advisor to the late Lord Aeloran. With his sharp features, silver hair, and piercing green eyes, Roland radiated an aura of authority and experience.

Unlike Eryndal and Soren, Roland had lived through centuries of conflict. He had fought in the Great War against Raxis and bore the scars of countless battles. The death of Lord Aeloran, his mentor and friend, had reignited a fire within him—a desire not just for vengeance, but to ensure that no more lives would be lost to the creeping darkness.

Roland's voice was steady and deliberate as he addressed the gathering. "The sigil of the serpent is no mere symbol," he said, his gaze sweeping over the assembled representatives. "It is a message and a warning. Aeloran believed it to be tied to ancient rituals—rituals designed to channel dark magic on a scale we have not seen since Raxis's fall. I failed my lord in life, but I will not fail him in death. We must act before it is too late."

The Realisation

As the three shared their findings, a grim realisation began to take shape. The murders of the elders and the strange occurrences across the land were not isolated incidents. They were deliberate acts carried out by a shadowy network—followers of Raxis who had operated in secret for centuries.

Eryndal's hands tightened into fists as Roland explained further. "These acolytes are performing rituals to resurrect Raxis, drawing upon forbidden magic and the blood of the realm's most powerful leaders. Each sigil is a key, part of an ancient and esoteric spell designed to rebind Raxis's fragmented soul to a physical form."

Soren nodded in agreement; her expression grim. "The serpent devouring its own tail—it is a symbol of eternity, of cycles. Raxis's acolytes are using these rituals to bridge the gap between life and death, ensuring that his essence can return to this world. And they are targeting us, the leaders of the four races because our blood holds the power to fuel their magic."

Eryndal felt a chill run down his spine. The serpent sigil was no longer just a mark of terror; it was a methodical tool of resurrection. He thought of his father, of the branded sigil on his chest, and realised the horrifying truth: Thalion's death had been part of this dark plan.

A Pact Forged in Shadows

Though their meeting was born of tragedy, it became clear that their shared purpose could not be ignored. The representatives of the four races, driven by grief and determination, agreed to pool their resources and knowledge.

Eryndal, despite his youth, stepped forward to address the group. "My father always believed in the strength of unity," he said, his voice steady despite the weight in his heart. "Raxis's followers seek to divide us, to weaken us through fear and mistrust. But if we stand together—humans, faes, elves, and gnomes—we can fight back. We can stop them before they complete their dark work."

Soren regarded him thoughtfully, her golden eyes searching his face. "You have your father's spirit," she said softly. "And his courage. If we are to succeed, we will need both."

Roland placed a hand on Eryndal's shoulder, a gesture of solidarity. "You have my sword, young lord. And my experience. Together, we may yet have a chance."

The pact was forged. Eryndal, Soren, and Roland would lead the effort to uncover and dismantle the shadowy network of Raxis's followers. But they knew the road ahead would be perilous.

A Glimpse into the Darkness

As the gathering concluded, a messenger arrived in the Hollow, pale and trembling. He brought news that chilled the assembled leaders to their cores.

In the distant Reldadan Mountains, the villagers below had reported an unnatural storm—a swirling vortex of black clouds that crackled with red lightning. The storm had not moved for days, hovering ominously over the ruins of an ancient fortress long forgotten by history. Witnesses claimed to hear whispers emanating from the storm, voices that spoke of vengeance and power.

Soren's gaze hardened. "The fortress lies near the border of the Heartwood, high up in the Reldadan Mountains."

Eryndal turned to Roland. "Do you know anything of this fortress? Could it be tied to Raxis?"

Roland's expression darkened. "It is said that Raxis once had a stronghold there, a place where he conducted his most forbidden experiments. If the storm lingers, it may be a sign that his essence is stirring, drawn to a place that was once his."

The Stirring of the Dark Lord

Though his body had been destroyed in the **Battle of the Broken Crown**, Raxis's soul had not been vanquished. Sealed in the Veil of Seraphran, his spirit had lingered, waiting for his acolytes to complete the rituals that would restore him to the mortal plane. Now, those rituals were happening all over Reldad.

Evidence of their dark work began to surface

- In the **Tivrah Desert**, travellers spoke of unearthly lights and shadowed figures moving beneath the dunes.
- Along the Bershian Coast, fishermen vanished without a trace, and strange chanting could be heard carried by the wind.
- The Mithran Valley's once-verdant fields became twisted and barren, the earth poisoned by tendrils of dark magic.

The three heroes stood amidst the circle of relics, the symbols of unity between humans, faes, elves and gnomes. It was here that Lyhterian Kael, the Chief Chronicler of Elderion, arrived bearing the weight of history in his arms. Clad in deep emerald robes embroidered with runes of knowledge, Lyhterian's every step echoed the importance of his mission. He approached the heroes, his expression grave yet determined, the weathered tomes clutched tightly to his chest. "These texts," he began, his voice rich and steady, "come from the depths of the Elderion Citadels's royal library. They hold truths that even the king and queens of Reldad have not dared speak aloud."

Carefully, he placed the ancient books on a stone pedestal etched with the sigils of the four races. The covers, made of enchanted leather and gilded in fading gold, bore the seal of the Magisterium—the council of sorcerers who had once fought alongside Thalion Bethkalen against the forces of darkness.

Eryndal's gaze flickered to the sigil, his heart heavy with the weight of the unknown. "What do they reveal?" He asked. Lyhterain opened the first tome, its pages glowing faintly as the runes shifted to a language the heroes could understand.

"They recount the rise of Raxis and the creation of the Black Nexus," he said. "The Black Nexus is not merely a place. It is a convergence of ley lines—rivers of magical energy that flow beneath our world. When these lines intersect, they create a focal point of unparalleled power. It was at the heart of the Nexus that Raxis performed his darkest rituals and where his soul, fractured by Thalion's spell, could be reconstituted."

Soren, her brows furrowing, traced the map drawn on one of the pages. The ley lines formed a chaotic web across Reldad and beyond, but at the centre lay a single ominous mark. "Where is this Black Nexus?" She asked.

Lytherian hesitated, his elven grace faltering for a moment. "Its exact location was hidden, even from the Magisterium, to prevent anyone from ever using its power again. But there are whispers—ancient hints—that it lies beyond the Bershian Sea, in a land where magic itself bends to the will of those who wield it." Lytherian continued, "The Black Nexus is the key to Raxis' resurrection although it is said there are other objects that are required to make his soul complete again."

The room grew heavy with this revelation. The Hollow of Accord, once a sanctuary of hope and unity, now felt like the staging ground for a battle that would decide the fate of the world. Lytherian closed the tome with a solemn sigh. "These texts are now yours. They are a map to understanding your enemy, but they are also a warning. The Black Nexus is a place of corruption. Even approaching it could test the limits of your resolve and your hearts." Eryndal, Soren and Roland exchanged glances, each knowing the role they had to play in saving Reldad. Lytherian inclined his head. " May the light of Eledrion guide your path and may the bonds of the Alliance hold strong."

As they prepared to depart, the Hollow of Accord seemed to hum with a quiet strength, as if the relics of old recognised the gravity of the moment. The path ahead was fraught with danger, but it was now clear; the fight against Raxis was not just for their world—it was for the very essence of magic itself. Eryndal looked to the horizon, his heart heavy but resolute. He carried the memory of his father and the weight of his people's hopes. For years, he had dismissed the warnings of the past. Now, he understood the truth: **the past was not dead. It had been waiting, just as Raxis had been. And now, it was his turn to rise and meet the challenge.**

A Kingdom on the Brink

Their journey would not only be a race against time but also a battle to hold the fractured alliances of the four races together. The unity that had once been their greatest strength during the Great War was now a fragile thing, frayed by centuries of mistrust and the recent murders that had targeted leaders from each race.

The gnomes had retreated into their underground kingdoms, wary of outsiders and unwilling to expose themselves to further attacks. The faes, shaken by the breach of their forest's magical barriers, questioned whether the other races could still be trusted to uphold the ancient pacts. The elves, grieving the loss of Lord Aeloran, had turned inward, their new leaders hesitant to commit to any course of action without proof of success.

Even among the humans, doubt lingered. Many questioned whether Eryndal, so young and untested, could fill his father's shoes and lead them in a fight against a foe as terrifying as Raxis.

As the three companions left the Hollow of Accord, Soren turned to Eryndal, her golden eyes piercing. "You know they doubt you," she said, her tone direct but not unkind.

"I know," Eryndal replied, his voice steady. "But doubt doesn't matter. Action does. My father believed in unity, and I will honour that belief. If I have to prove myself to them along the way, so be it."

Roland, who had been silently sharpening his blade, looked up with a rare glint of approval in his eyes. "You have more steel in you than I thought, boy. Let's hope it's enough."

The return of Raxis was no longer a question of *if*. It was only a matter of *when*.

With the land of Reldad trembling on the edge of chaos, Eryndal, Soren, and Roland became the kingdom's last hope. To stop the dark resurrection of Raxis, they would need to travel to the farthest corners of the realm, uncover its most dangerous secrets, and confront the growing shadow before it consumed the world.

But as they set out into the unknown, one truth lingered in their hearts: the battle against Raxis had never truly ended. It had only been postponed.

Chapter 4
The Alliance of the Heart

The dawn of their journey cast golden light across the land of Reldad, illuminating the beauty and scars of a world on the brink of chaos. Rolling hills stretched into dense forests, their emerald canopy punctuated by jagged peaks that pierced the morning mist. Between these landscapes lay the fractured realms of the faes, elves, gnomes, and humans—once united under the banner of the **Alliance of the Heart**, now divided by years of complacency and distrust.

For Eryndal Bethkalen, Soren Daliath Redborn, and Roland Thorne Bardin, the weight of the past and the burden of the future rested heavily on their shoulders. If they were to have any hope of stopping Raxis's resurrection, they would first need to rebuild the Alliance. What had once been a beacon of hope and unity against a common enemy had faded into a distant memory, eroded by decades of peace that had allowed suspicion to fester.

Eryndal had seen this fragility firsthand at the **Hollow of Accord**, where representatives from each race had gathered in response to the murders. Accusations had flown like arrows, tempers had flared, and the fragile unity had unravelled before his eyes. Now, as they stood at the precipice of their dangerous quest, the three heroes knew that rekindling the Alliance of the Heart would be their first and perhaps greatest challenge.

The History of the Alliance

The Alliance of the Heart had been forged generations ago during the Great War, a desperate response to the terror unleashed by Raxis. It had been more than a mere coalition of armies—it was a symbol of hope, a vow that the four races would stand together to protect their world from annihilation. Leaders of each realm had sworn the **Oath of Unity**, binding their peoples to a pact of mutual aid and shared purpose.

Through combined strength, the Alliance had achieved what no single race could: the defeat of Raxis and the sealing of his soul within the Veil of Seraphran. Yet, as years turned to decades, the hard-fought bonds had begun to fray. The faes retreated deeper into their enchanted forests, their wards shielding them from the outside world. The elves, long-lived and wary, grew detached, content to observe the affairs of the mortal world from afar. The gnomes, ever industrious, focused inward, building wonders beneath the earth but growing isolated in the process. Meanwhile, the humans—short-lived and ambitious—expanded their borders, often to the irritation of their neighbours.

Now, with the return of Raxis's influence threatening all they had built, the once-proud Alliance was little more than a relic of the past.

The Challenges Ahead

"We'll never stop Raxis if we can't even trust each other," Soren had said as they prepared to leave the Hollow of Accord. Her voice, though calm, carried an edge of frustration. The fae emissary had seen how fear and blame had consumed the gathering, each race accusing the others of failing to prevent the rising darkness.

Eryndal nodded grimly. "If the leaders of the four races can't see what's at stake, we'll make them see." His words carried the conviction of a man determined to honour his father's memory, but even he knew the enormity of the task before them.

Roland, the elven warrior who had seen more centuries than he cared to count, had been less optimistic. "Unity is a blade that dulls quickly when there's no war to sharpen it," he had said. "We can try to forge it anew, but it won't be easy."

Their plan was ambitious and fraught with peril. They would travel to the heart of each realm, appealing directly to the leaders of the faes, elves, gnomes, and humans. They would need to mend fractured relationships, address old grievances, and convince each race that the threat of Raxis was not just a human concern but a danger to all.

The First Steps

The journey began in the heart of the fae lands, a realm of untamed beauty and ethereal magic. Shimmering forests stretched endlessly towards the horizon, their ancient trees glowing faintly in hues of green and silver as if infused with moonlight. Rivers wound their way through the glades, their waters sparkling with otherworldly light, carrying faint echoes of melodies long forgotten by mortal ears. This was the domain of the faes, a race deeply attuned to nature, whose magic was as much a part of the land as the roots of the great Eldertrees.

For Soren Daliath Redborn, the faes' lands were both a sanctuary and a source of unease. She had grown up amidst the whispering trees and glowing rivers, but her years spent beyond the forest's protective wards had distanced her from the traditions and hierarchies that now defined her people. Even as they approached the towering sanctuary of **Tirforessa Perioth**, queen of the faes, Soren hesitated.

"This is your home," Eryndal said, noticing her hesitation. "Surely your queen will listen."

"She'll listen," Soren replied, her voice steady, though her hands betrayed a slight tremor. "But the faes do not rush to action. Convincing Tirforessa to act—and to trust the others—will be harder than you think."

Eryndal nodded, glancing towards Roland, who stood silently behind them. The elven warrior's stoicism belied his unease. "Then let's make our case, together."

The Court of Eldertree

Tirforessa's sanctuary, the **Court of Eldertree**, was a marvel even to those who had spent their lives within the fae lands. The great Eldertree stood at the heart of the court, its trunk so vast that entire halls and chambers had been carved into its bark. Light emanated softly from the tree itself, casting the court in a perpetual glow that felt both otherworldly and comforting. Fae nobles, adorned in shimmering garments that seemed to shift colours with every step, gathered in curious silence as the three heroes approached.

Queen Tirforessa sat on a throne of living branches, her presence commanding yet serene. Her long, silver hair flowed like liquid light, and her eyes, a piercing shade of emerald, seemed to see through Soren's carefully composed demeanour.

"Soren Redborn," the queen said, her voice like the rustling of leaves. "You have returned, though not without purpose, it seems. Speak."

Soren knelt, her companions following suit. "Your Majesty, the balance of our world is in danger. Raxis's followers move openly once more. They have already claimed the lives of leaders across Reldad, leaving the serpent sigil in their wake. The signs of his growing power are unmistakable. If we do not act together, the Veil of Seraphran will fall, and Raxis will return."

The queen's expression darkened, but her gaze remained fixed on Soren. "The affairs of the other races have long brought ruin to our lands. Why should we risk ourselves again? The faes have endured, protected by our own wards and vigilance. Why must we now entangle ourselves in their chaos?"

Before Soren could respond, Eryndal stepped forward. "Because this darkness will not stop at your borders. My father gave his life trying to warn us of what was coming. I won't let his sacrifice be for nothing, but I can't do this without your help."

Tirforessa's sharp eyes turned to Eryndal, and for a long moment, silence reigned. Finally, the queen spoke, "Your words carry weight, young warrior, but the faes do not act on words alone. If this Alliance is to be rekindled, the other races must also pledge their aid. Only then will we lend our strength."

Though her agreement was conditional, it was enough to give them hope. As the queen's court dissolved into quiet murmurs, Soren exhaled a breath she hadn't realised she was holding. Their first step was complete, but the path ahead was far from certain.

The Gnome Kingdom of Aetherdeep

From the glowing forests of the faes, the trio turned westward, travelling for days across rocky terrain until the peaks of the **Aether Mountains** loomed before them. Beneath these mountains lay the gnome kingdom of **Aetherdeep**, a sprawling network of underground cities known for their engineering marvels and labyrinthine design.

The journey into Aetherdeep was not an easy one. The air grew colder as they climbed into the mountains, and the path was fraught with treacherous terrain. At last, they reached the **Gates of Iron**, towering constructs that marked the entrance to the gnome city.

Gnomes, small in stature but fierce in their ingenuity, greeted the trio with scepticism. They were led through winding tunnels, their walls inlaid with glowing veins of mithril, until they reached the central chamber of Aetherdeep: a grand hall filled with the hum of machinery and the chatter of gnomish inventors. At its centre stood **Kinzo Macerald**, the gruff and pragmatic leader of the gnomes.

Kinzo wasted no time on pleasantries. "Outsiders don't come here without reason. Speak your business and be quick about it."

Roland stepped forward, his voice steady and calm. "Your tunnels are shaking. Your leaders are dying. The signs of Raxis's return are all around us, and they will not spare you. You've seen it before, and you'll see it again—unless we stand together."

Kinzo's eyes narrowed, his expression unreadable. "Bold words, Elf. But the gnomes are not so easily swayed. If what you say is true, then show us proof. Bring us something we can hold, something we can see. Until then, we'll keep our strength for ourselves."

Eryndal's frustration threatened to boil over, but Soren placed a hand on his arm, her gaze steady. "We'll bring you proof," she said. "And when we do, I trust you'll keep your word."

Kinzo nodded gruffly, his attention already shifting back to the intricate mechanisms on his desk.

A Call for Help

As the trio left Aetherdeep, their minds were heavy with the challenges ahead. The faes had agreed in principle but demanded the support of the other races. The gnomes were willing to listen, but only if provided with irrefutable proof of Raxis's resurgence. And now they turned their sights eastward, towards the Elves of **Valithor**, a golden city perched high in the cliffs of the **Eastern Mountains**.

Their journey to Valithor took them through the **Silverwood Glade**, where moonlight filtered through the trees in a dazzling display of light and shadow. It was here, beneath the ancient boughs, that Eryndal finally voiced the doubts that had been weighing on him.

"We can't do this alone," he said, his voice quiet but firm.

Soren and Roland turned to him, their faces questioning.

"Even if the Alliance holds, Raxis is stronger now," Eryndal continued. "We'll need more than diplomacy to stop him. There are stories—of relics, artefacts, and people with gifts like ours. If we're going to win this, we need to find them."

Roland nodded; his expression thoughtful. "The old tales speak of such things: a golden amulet said to ward off the darkest magic, an ancient sword forged to pierce the hearts of sorcerers. If they exist, they could tip the balance."

Soren frowned but said nothing. She had heard the stories too, but she knew the cost of chasing myths. Still, the weight of Eryndal's words lingered as they continued their journey.

The Elves of Valithor

Valithor, the shining city of the elves, was a sight to behold. Its golden spires rose from the cliffs like rays of sunlight made solid, their surfaces etched with intricate patterns that seemed to glow with an inner light. But beneath the city's splendour lay a people divided by grief and uncertainty.

The death of Lord Aeloran had left the elves without a clear leader, and Queen **Enareth Bonafin**, though wise and commanding, faced dissent among her people. When the trio was brought before her, they could feel the tension in the air.

Eryndal spoke first, recounting the serpent sigil and the growing signs of Raxis's return. When he mentioned the death of his father, Enareth's expression softened.

"The sigil of the serpent," she murmured, her voice laced with memory. "We thought it was gone forever."

"It's back," Eryndal said firmly. "And so is Raxis. If we don't unite now, none of us will survive what's coming."

Enareth's gaze lingered on Eryndal, her sharp eyes weighing his words.

Finally, she nodded. "The elves will stand with the Alliance. But know this: we are not the force we once were. If Raxis is truly rising, we will need time to prepare."

The Path Ahead

With the faes, gnomes, and elves tentatively aligned, the Alliance of the Heart had begun to take shape. But the road ahead was long and fraught with peril. As the three heroes prepared to leave Valithor, Eryndal's words from earlier haunted them all.

If they were to stop Raxis, they would need more than alliances. They would need power, and the whispered tales of ancient relics and forgotten allies would drive them forward into the unknown.

The wind carried with it a chilling whisper, a shadow of Raxis's growing presence. Time was running out.

Chapter 5
The Stonguard

The **Forest of the Faes** whispered in a language older than words, the trees shifting as though alive, bending their branches to listen to the wind's secrets. A thick silver fog clung to the ground, illuminated by shafts of pale moonlight filtering through the ancient canopy. The hum of magic was palpable here, flowing through every root and leaf.

Eryndal Bethkalen sat by the crackling campfire, running a whetstone over the edge of his sword. The rhythmic hiss of metal against stone was a comforting ritual, though his mind was anything but calm. His eyes strayed to the shadows beyond the firelight. Soren Daliath Redborn had disappeared over an hour ago, slipping into the forest with a purpose she hadn't shared.

"She's been gone too long," Eryndal said, his tone clipped.

Roland Thorne Bardin leaned against a nearby tree, his elven eyes trained on the dark horizon. "This is her land," he said simply. "She knows it better than either of us."

"That doesn't mean she's safe," Eryndal muttered.

Roland offered a faint smile, though his hand never strayed far from his bow. "You worry too much, Bethkalen. The forest is as much her ally as you are."

Before Eryndal could reply, a low, melodic hum drifted through the trees, stopping both men in their tracks. It was faint at first, a haunting melody that seemed to ripple through the air like a living thing.

"What is that?" Eryndal asked, rising to his feet.

Roland tilted his head, listening. His sharp hearing picked out the rhythm of words buried in the sound, and his expression grew serious. "It's a language. An old one."

Eryndal's brow furrowed. "Old how?"

Roland's gaze turned to him. "Older than the kingdoms. Older than the Alliance. I've heard it before—once, during the blessings of Aravell's soil."

Eryndal's pulse quickened. The melody stirred a memory deep within him —a memory he had nearly forgotten, tucked away in the recesses of his mind. His father had used that same tongue—whispers of it in the nights after his training when he was young and still learning of the old magic that had shaped their family's destiny. **The Ancient Tongue**, as his father called it. It was a language of power and old pacts, long lost to most except for a few who still carried the weight of those forgotten words.

Eryndal swallowed hard. "That can't be…"

Roland, ever the pragmatic warrior, was already moving towards the source of the sound, his bow in hand and ready for anything. "We don't have time to speculate. Let's go."

Without a word, Eryndal followed, his hand tightening around the hilt of his sword as the air grew colder, heavier with magic. They pushed deeper into the forest, the trees parting slightly to reveal a clearing ahead where the moonlight seemed unnaturally bright. In the centre of the clearing, there knelt **Soren**, her arms raised, her voice an ethereal echo as she spoke those ancient words. She was facing a creature—a thing of stone and flame.

The beast stood easily twelve feet tall, its body formed of smooth, polished boulders, veined with glowing blue cracks that pulsed with an inner light. Its wings, jagged and immense, unfurled with a slow, deliberate motion. The wings were like those of a dragon—sharp-edged and woven with an arcane energy that crackled and snapped. Its eyes blazed with a fierce, intelligent fire, locking onto Soren with an almost reverent gaze.

Eryndal's breath caught in his throat. "What is that?"

Soren did not look back, her voice still carrying that same haunting cadence. "This is a **Stonguard**," she said, almost matter-of-factly.

"A **what**?" Eryndal asked, his mind racing.

Soren stood slowly, her fingers brushing against the creature's rough, rocky hide. "A **Stonguard**. Ancient protectors of the fae. They were bound by an old enchantment, one that my people used to summon when the world stood on the brink of destruction."

Eryndal's mind raced, piecing together the fragments of his father's old tales—stories of creatures bound to ancient pacts, protectors born of the earth itself. But this. this was something else entirely.

The creature shifted, its massive wings folding against its back with a deep rumble, and it bowed its head before Soren. "You can speak to it?" Eryndal asked, his voice trembling slightly with disbelief.

"I speak the Ancient Tongue, yes," Soren replied, turning to face him now, her eyes glinting with something unreadable. "And the Stonguard answer to that language. Only the fae can summon them. The bond is as old as the first fae kingdom, and the Stonguard have stood vigilant ever since."

Eryndal's mind spun. He had no idea how powerful the bond between Soren and the Stonguard truly was. But seeing it before him, feeling the power in the air, was enough to understand: this creature was no mere guardian. It was a force of nature, older than most of the world itself, and bound by an oath that could not be broken.

Before he could ask more questions, a harsh whistle cut through the night, sharp and deliberate. Roland's voice came low, urgent. "We're not alone."

The three of them immediately tensed, the Stonguard's head snapping towards the source of the sound. Without hesitation, they moved swiftly through the trees, the glow from the Stonguard's veins lighting their path. They reached the edge of the clearing and found the source of the disturbance: five hooded figures standing in a circle, their low chants resonating through the air like dark incantations.

The magic was palpable—thick and twisted, woven with an ancient, dark energy that seemed to choke the very air around them. Eryndal felt the hairs on the back of his neck rise as the symbols they chanted in unison began to swirl in the air, inscribed with the sigil of a serpent devouring its own tail—the mark of **Raxis**.

"What are they doing?" Roland hissed under his breath, not taking his eyes off the ritual.

"Calling to him," Soren replied, her voice cold with disgust. "They're summoning Raxis's influence. They want to see him rise again."

Eryndal's stomach twisted. "Isn't that…"

Before he could finish, one of the figures raised her head, her eyes flashing with an unnatural gleam. "We're not alone," the figure said, her voice a hiss that seemed to echo in every direction.

The chant stopped abruptly.

The figure's hood fell back, revealing a face both striking and terrifying—a woman with angular features and eyes as black as void. Her gaze locked onto Eryndal, and an ice-cold chill spread through him, deeper than mere fear. He recognised her immediately.

"**Morva Sable**," Roland whispered, his voice a low growl. "Impossible. She was—"

"Dead, yes," Soren finished for him. "Everyone thought she was dead after the Battle of the Broken Crown. But it seems we were wrong."

Morva Sable's lips curled into a cold, serpentine smile. "So, the **heroes** return. How…predictable."

Before either Eryndal or Roland could move, Morva raised a hand, and a burst of dark energy exploded from her palm, sending the heroes sprawling backwards. The Stonguard roared in fury, stepping between Morva and the heroes, but she did not falter. With another wave of her hand, the Stonguard staggered backwards, its fiery eyes flickering with dissonance as if the dark magic was reaching its very essence.

"**Morva!**" Soren cried, stepping forward, her voice ringing with ancient power as she spoke the words of the

Ancient Tongue. The Stonguard responded with a low, rumbling growl, its wings flaring, but Morva's eyes flashed with a dark light.

In a flash of movement too quick for the eye to follow, Morva vanished. Her form disintegrated into a mist, swirling around them before vanishing entirely, leaving only the scent of burning ash in the air.

The Stonguard let out an earth-shaking roar, searching the trees for any sign of the woman. But there was nothing. Morva had disappeared into the shadows.

Eryndal shook his head, breathless. "Where—how did she—"

Soren's voice was low; her eyes narrowed. "She is a master of illusions and dark magic. That woman. She is no mere follower. She's one of **Raxis's** strongest lieutenants. And her death was a lie. One we've all been fed."

Roland's jaw tightened. "This isn't over. We can't let her escape."

But as they began to move forward, the remaining followers, four in total, stepped back, clearly terrified. Their faces were pale, eyes wide, and trembling from the overwhelming presence of the Stonguard. Soren, her voice hard, ordered them to stand down.

"You will speak," she said, her tone unwavering, "or your deaths will be far slower than you imagine."

The four captives exchanged terrified glances, but their defiance faltered under the Stonguard's fiery gaze. After a long pause, one of them—an older man—finally dropped to his knees. "Raxis lives," he whispered, his voice breaking. "The serpent sigil is returning. His followers are gathering, and his power…his power is growing."

The truth hung heavy in the air. Soren turned to Eryndal and Roland, her eyes filled with a mixture of determination and concern. "We have our proof. It is time to confront the truth. Raxis is coming. And we must act before it's too late."

As they marched the captives through the forest towards the gnomes' kingdom, the air felt thicker with the weight of the knowledge they now carried. The Stonguard remained vigilant, its massive form casting a shadow over them, ever-watchful and ready to strike at any who dared oppose their mission.

Eryndal's thoughts were heavy as they continued their journey. Morva's return was a harbinger of dark things to come. And Raxis, no matter the odds, would not be stopped easily. Yet there was one thing that remained in his mind—despite the darkness, despite the danger: **They were not alone**.

Arriving in Boulderdeep, Kinzo sat upon his throne, carved with intricate runes of gnomish heritage, his sharp eyes fixed on the trembling captives. His voice cut through the heavy silence like a blade. "Proof," he demanded, his tone unyielding. "I need undeniable proof of Raxis' return."

One of the captives, his body quivering under the relentless glare of the Stonguard, finally broke. "Morva Sable lives," he choked out, his voice barely above a whisper, "She walks among us, gathering his forces. The serpent sigil...it has returned."

The chamber grew deathly silent, the weight of the revelation pressing down on all present. Even the air seemed to still as Kinzo leaned forward, his expression hardening with grim resolve. "The Alliance of the Heart is no longer a matter of debate," he declared, his voice echoing off the ancient stone walls. "It is a necessity. If Morva Sable truly walks this world once more, then Raxis' return is imminent, we must act swiftly, or all will be lost."

Soren stepped forward; her voice steady yet urgent. "Then we must move quickly. First to the humans—they are the keystone of the Alliance. Without their commitment, the unity of the races will falter." Kinzo nodded solemnly. "Humans have always been proud and slow to trust. Convincing them will not be easy. They will demand more than words and captives to sway them." Roland crossed his arms, his expression dark, "Then we will bring them whether they need—truth and action. If they can't see the threat now, they will when it reaches their gates."

As the Stonguard hauled the captives away, Soren turned to Eryndal, her eyes filled with a quiet intensity. "This journey isn't just about uniting the Alliance. It's about showing the world that you're not just Thalion's son—you are his legacy. If anyone can bring the races together, it's you." Eryndal nodded, his hand gripping the hilt of his staff tightly. He felt the weight of his father's name. The Alliance was more than a call to arms; it was a chance to preserve everything his father had sacrificed for.

As they prepared to leave the gnome kingdom, the gravity of their mission settled heavily on their shoulders. They would head to the lands of the humans, to seek their aid in reforging the bonds that once saved Reldad. The three heroes exchanged grim yet determined looks as they stepped into the cold mountain air. The journey to the human kingdom awaited them, a vital step towards reuniting the Alliance of the Heart. Time was running out, and with Morva Sable's dark magic spreading across the lands, they knew their task was only beginning.

Chapter 6
The Binding of the Alliance

The call to reform the **Alliance of the Heart** echoed far beyond the borders of Aldenrow, summoning the Magisterium from their floating city of **Aetherion**, a marvel of magical engineering and ancient wisdom. Suspended above the shimmering Lake Viridian, Aetherion was home to the twelve most powerful sorcerers in the human realm. It served as a sanctuary of arcane knowledge and the seat of magical authority, where the Magisterium governed the arcane affairs of the land and safeguarded the delicate balance between mortal life and the mystical forces that surrounded it.

To call the Magisterium down from Aetherion was no small matter. Their presence signified a moment of profound importance, for they rarely left their floating city unless the fate of the world itself hung in the balance. Answering Eryndal's summons, the twelve sorcerers descended to Aldenrow, drawn by the gravity of the request to reform the Alliance. It was their duty to bear witness to the rekindling of this ancient bond and, more importantly, to determine if the situation warranted their ultimate authority: the granting of the **Seal of the Alliance**, an enchantment of unparalleled power that could only be invoked with their unanimous consent.

Aetherion Descends

The arrival of the Magisterium was heralded by whispers of awe and unease. As twilight fell over Aldenrow, a faint glow appeared in the sky, growing brighter as Aetherion descended from the heavens. The floating city was a wonder of polished stone and crystalline spires, its base adorned with runes that pulsed with radiant energy. Great chains of light anchored it to the ground, tethering the ethereal city to the mortal plane for the duration of the Magisterium's stay.

The citizens of Aldenrow gathered in the shadow of the **Grand Oak**, watching in silence as the Magisterium emerged from their shimmering portal at the city's edge. Each sorcerer walked with an air of majesty and authority, their robes glinting with the sigils of their respective domains. They proceeded in solemn formation towards the ancient tree, where Eryndal, Soren, and Roland awaited them.

The Gathering Beneath the Grand Oak

Under the massive canopy of the Grand Oak, the Magisterium formed their circle of power, their twelve seats carved from the same enchanted wood as the tree itself. Elder Halveth, their leader, took his place at the northernmost seat, flanked by Elder Celestine, mistress of divination, and Elder Maldrin, the keeper of elemental fire. Each sorcerer carried a staff or talisman of their choosing, symbols of their mastery over their respective arts.

Eryndal stepped forward, feeling the weight of their collective gaze. The Magisterium's presence was overwhelming; each sorcerer radiated an aura of power that seemed to warp the air around them.

Halveth was the first to speak, his deep, resonant voice echoing through the gathering. "We, the Magisterium of Aetherion, have heard your summons, Eryndal Bethkalen. You claim that the Alliance of the Heart must be reforged and that the ancient seal must be invoked once more. These are no trivial requests. Speak now and let us judge the truth of your words."

The Plea for Unity

Eryndal began, his voice steady despite the enormity of the moment. "Honoured elders of the Magisterium, I come before you not as a warrior or a son of Thalion, but as a steward of Reldad's future. The signs are undeniable—Raxis's followers are rising again. The serpent sigil has reappeared, carved into the flesh of our leaders. His acolytes perform dark rituals across the land, seeking to unbind his soul from the Veil of Seraphran. If we do not act now, Raxis will return to plunge our world into darkness."

The Magisterium listened in silence; their faces impassive. Elder Celestine's sharp eyes flicked to Soren and Roland. "And these companions of yours? Do they also vouch for the truth of your claims?"

Soren stepped forward, her fae presence captivating. "I am Soren Daliath Redborn, sent by my queen to uncover the truth behind the shadow rising in Reldad. I have seen its signs firsthand—the twisted corruption of the ley lines, the desecration of sacred places. Raxis is not a threat to humans alone. He seeks to dominate all life. If the Alliance does not stand united, none of us will survive."

Roland followed, his voice steady and calm. "I am Roland Thorne Bardin, once advisor to Lord Aeloran of the elves. My people have suffered greatly at the hands of Raxis's followers. I swore an oath to protect this land, and I stand here now to honour that oath. Eryndal speaks the truth. The Alliance of the Heart is our only hope."

The Magisterium's Scepticism

Halveth stroked his long silver beard, his expression contemplative. "Your words carry the weight of conviction, but the Magisterium cannot act on passion alone. The Seal of the Alliance is no mere spell—it binds the hearts and fates of the four races, as it did in the days of your father. To invoke it without cause is to risk unbalancing the very fabric of the world. What proof do you bring to us of Raxis's return?"

Eryndal gestured to Soren, who produced a bundle wrapped in cloth. She unveiled a charred wooden medallion engraved with the serpent sigil of Raxis, its edges still faintly glowing with dark magic. "This was taken from the site of a ritual in the fae lands. The blood of my kin was spilt to empower it. The energy radiating from this artefact is unmistakable—Raxis's acolytes are working to break the seals that bind his soul."

The sorcerers murmured among themselves, their scepticism wavering. Elder Maldrin leaned forward, his fiery eyes narrowing. "This...this is no ordinary artefact. The magic within it is ancient and vile. If this is the work of Raxis's followers, then the threat is indeed grave."

The Invocation of the Seal

Halveth rose to his feet, his silver staff glinting in the sunlight. "If what you say is true, then the Alliance must be reforged. But to invoke the seal is not a decision we take lightly. The enchantment requires the unity of all four races, as it did in the days of Thalion. Each leader must pledge their people's hearts to the cause, and the Magisterium must grant its approval."

Soren spoke with urgency. "The faes have pledged their support. The elves and gnomes have also agreed, though they await your decision before they will fully commit."

Halveth's gaze swept over the other sorcerers, his voice solemn. "Then let us begin the ritual."

The Magisterium rose as one, forming a circle around the base of the Grand Oak. Their staves and talismans began to glow with brilliant light as they chanted in unison, their voices weaving a spell of incredible power. The air around the tree shimmered and vibrated as the enchantment took shape.

Eryndal, Soren, and Roland stood in the centre of the circle, their hands joined. The magic surged through them, binding their hearts and souls to the fate of the Alliance. The Grand Oak seemed to respond, its leaves glowing with golden light as its roots dug deeper into the earth, connecting with the ley lines of magic that stretched across Reldad.

When the ritual was complete, Halveth lowered his staff, his voice ringing with finality. "The Alliance of the Heart is reforged. May it hold strong in the face of the darkness to come."

As the gathered crowd erupted into cheers and prayers, Eryndal felt a renewed sense of purpose. The first step had been taken, but the true battle was only beginning.

Chapter 7
A Call to the Four Races

Eryndal stood on the balcony of Kinzo Macerald's great stone hall, overlooking the vast, glittering expanse of the gnome kingdom. Below him, the city sprawled like an intricate web, each stone structure carefully placed and meticulously crafted. The hum of gears turning and the distant rumbles of forge fires carried through the air. The scent of metal and stone mingled with the cool, crisp air that blew from the mountain heights. Yet, despite the industrious clamour of gnome society below, Eryndal's mind was far from the momentary tranquillity the view offered. His thoughts were consumed with the weight of their discovery: Morva Sable was alive, and Raxis's dark influence was stirring once more.

Though the Alliance of the Heart had been forged once again, and the seal of approval granted by the Magisterium, the challenge of their mission had only just begun. The task ahead—to unify the races against a common threat—was more daunting than ever. And now, with the return of Morva and the growing presence of Raxis's dark power, Eryndal knew there was no time to waste. Every moment counted.

"The message must reach them all," Eryndal murmured to himself, eyes distant as the full magnitude of their task settled within him. The four races—elves, faes, humans, and gnomes—needed to know the truth of Morva Sable's return. They needed to know the gravity of the situation. And most urgently of all, they needed to understand that Raxis's return was no longer a distant threat. The darkness was growing, and time was running out.

He turned from the balcony as Soren and Roland entered the hall, their expressions grave. Both had stood by him through the long process of restoring the Alliance, through the long nights spent in council and the quiet assurances of the Magisterium. Now, the next step in their mission was clear: They needed to send word to each of the races, and they needed to do so with the utmost urgency.

"We've been granted the seal," Eryndal began, his voice resolute as he met the eyes of his companions. "The Alliance of the Heart is reformed; the Magisterium has given its approval. But that won't matter if we can't stop Raxis's return. The message we carry needs to reach the four corners of Reldad. The leaders must know the truth, and they must be ready."

Soren nodded in agreement, her silver hair shimmering faintly under the dim light of the hall. Her gaze turned to the gathered creatures; each one chosen for the task ahead.

"The time for waiting is over," Soren said, her voice a steady echo of the urgency that lay heavy in the air. "We have to act now. If we don't reach them in time—"

"We will reach them," Eryndal interrupted firmly, his eyes narrowing with determination. "The Alliance is strong, but they need to know the full extent of what's happening. Morva Sable's survival is proof enough that Raxis is close to returning. We need the four races to stand together, not just in name, but in strength."

Roland stepped forward; his expression grim yet focused. "We'll have the message delivered. We've chosen the right creatures. Each one is sacred to their race, a symbol of trust and loyalty. They'll get the word to the leaders. And then we can prepare for what's coming."

Eryndal turned his attention to the creatures before them—each one an embodiment of their race's power and significance, chosen to carry their message to the four corners of the realm.

The Messengers of the Four Races

Eryndal stood, his gaze fixed on the four sacred creatures gathered before him, their eyes filled with intelligence and purpose. These were no ordinary animals; each one had been carefully chosen for its strength, its symbolism, and its deep, ancient connection to the four races. These messengers were more than mere carriers of information—they were living representations of their peoples' magic, power, and resilience. Their role in this momentous task was critical. With Raxis's shadow looming over the world, the bond between the races had never been more important. If the message they carried was to be received with the urgency it demanded, these creatures would ensure it reached its destination in a way no other being could.

Each of these messengers was more than capable of completing their mission—they were the embodiment of their race's hopes, history, and strength.

1. The Elves: The Starlit Eagle

The **starlit eagle**, a creature that could soar as easily through the heavens as it could through the hearts of the elves, was one of the most revered beings in elven society. Its feathers shimmered like the night sky itself, streaked with silver and gold, casting a faint, celestial glow as it flew. Its wings were not just instruments of flight but extensions of the stars—the same stars that the elves had studied and revered for millennia. The eagle's magic was ancient, as old as the elves themselves, and it carried the wisdom of the cosmos within its very bones.

The starlit eagle was not only a messenger but a protector, a symbol of the elven race's grace and intellect. For generations, it had carried the words of **Queen Enareth Boneftine**, delivering commands, decrees, and messages of utmost importance across the sprawling forests of Valithor. Now, it was chosen to carry a far graver message. Its flight would be swift and seamless as it traversed the ancient forests of Reldad, its glowing feathers leaving a trail that would be seen only by those who were meant to witness it.

The eagle's keen sight allowed it to find the hidden paths through the elven lands, ensuring no obstacle—be it the thickest of woodlands or the most treacherous of cliffs—could slow it down. Its bond with the elves was unparalleled; it could read the stars as easily as it could understand the ancient magic that flowed through its wings. The starlit eagle would not only bear Eryndal's urgent message but also remind the elves of their deep connection to the cosmos and the role they must play in facing the darkness that threatened to consume the world.

2. The Faes: The Glimmer Fox

The **glimmer fox** was an embodiment of the fae's magical essence. Sleek and elusive, it moved with an agility and grace that made it nearly impossible to track, yet it always seemed to be present, its glowing fur leaving traces of light in the darkness of the faes' mystical forests. Its fur was bioluminescent, alive with shifting, intricate patterns that flickered like the lights of distant stars, and its eyes were the colour of the pale moon, glowing softly with an ancient knowledge only the faes could truly understand. It was a creature born of magic, attuned to the very pulse of the world around it.

For the faes, the glimmer fox was both a symbol of the fae's connection to the magical realms and a messenger capable of crossing between them. The fae had long relied on these creatures to carry messages between the realms of the living and the world of dreams, and the glimmer fox had been one of their most trusted allies. Its ability to slip between worlds made it invaluable—not only in delivering messages swiftly but also in ensuring that those messages were received with clarity, no matter where they were sent.

Soren had chosen the glimmer fox to carry the message to **Tirforessa Perioth** and **Tersio Fiprot**, the leaders of the faes in Luminara. Its ability to weave through the glowing trees of their crystalline groves, its form almost blending with the light itself, would ensure that the message arrived unnoticed by enemies but received by the fae in all its urgency. The glimmer fox was both a guide and a beacon, carrying the knowledge of the fae people to their leaders as they prepared for the inevitable war.

3. The Humans: The Midnight Stag

The **midnight stag** was a creature shrouded in mystery and majesty. Cloaked in the deepest black fur, it blended seamlessly into the night, its presence was often felt rather than seen. The stag's most striking feature, however, was its antlers—massive and branching like the very night sky itself, glowing faintly with starlight. These antlers were said to be imbued with ancient magic, capable of guiding the stag through the darkest of times and the most dangerous of terrains.

The midnight stag was not just a creature of beauty; it was a symbol of resilience and endurance. The humans of Reldad had revered the stag for generations, seeing it as both a guide and a protector. It was a creature that thrived in the darkest of forests, where danger lurked around every corner. Its silent, swift movements made it the perfect messenger in times of strife, able to traverse the plains and hills of human territories without making a sound. Its hooves, though powerful enough to crush stone, left no trace on the earth, ensuring its movements remained undetected.

For **King Valdran Delrad** of Harrowdale, the midnight stag was more than a symbol—it was a reminder of his people's ability to endure and fight back against the darkness. The stag would carry Eryndal's message through the human lands, from the great fortress city of Harrowdale to the furthest reaches of Reldad. Its journey would be one of both urgency and quiet determination, bearing the weight of an entire kingdom on its shoulders.

4. The Gnomes: The Stonehound

The **stonehound** was the very embodiment of the gnomes' ingenuity and tenacity. Carved from the very stone of Reldad's mountains, this creature was as solid and unyielding as the land it came from. Its body was made of rough-hewn stone, yet it moved with surprising grace, its muscular frame powered by gnome magic that bound the very rocks of the earth together. Its eyes glowed like molten lava, the light from within a reflection of the gnomes' deep connection to the core of the world and their ancient, earth-based magic.

The stonehound was not just a creature of strength—it was a symbol of endurance and resilience, as steadfast as the gnomes themselves. For generations, the gnomes had relied on creatures like the stonehound to protect their strongholds and to carry messages between their mountain cities and across the plains. The stonehound's ability to endure the harshest environments made it the ideal messenger for the gnomes, who inhabited some of the most dangerous and treacherous regions in Reldad.

Kinzo Macerald had chosen the stonehound to carry Eryndal's message across the gnome strongholds, from the peaks of the mountains to the deep caverns below. The stonehound would navigate the rocky cliffs and winding caves, its body hardened by centuries of evolution. It would deliver word to the furthest reaches of gnome territory, ensuring that the message of Raxis's return reached the gnome leaders and that they too would be ready to face the coming storm. The stonehound was more than just a creature of stone; it was a living testament to the gnomes' spirit, bound by both rock and magic to defend their world.

Each of these creatures was chosen not only for its ability to carry Eryndal's urgent message but for the deep, ancient connection it had to the very essence of the four races. These messengers were more than just symbols—they were the key to ensuring that the races of Reldad remained united in the face of the coming darkness.

Eryndal stood before them, the animals now ready, the scrolls of parchment containing his message tied securely to their backs. The time for discussion had passed. There was nothing left but to send them out into the world, where the fate of Reldad would be decided. Each creature was bonded to its race, an embodiment of trust and sacred duty. They were more than just messengers—they were the harbingers of hope and warning.

"Take the message," Eryndal said, his voice unwavering as he stepped back. "To the elves, to the faes, to the humans, and to the gnomes. Tell them what we have learned. Tell them that Morva Sable lives and that Raxis's return is imminent. We cannot wait any longer."

With final nods, the creatures departed in a whirlwind of motion. The glimmer fox vanished into the night, leaving behind only the faintest glow, while the midnight stag leapt into the air, its hooves barely grazing the ground as it made its way towards the distant mountains. The starlit eagle spread its wings, soaring high above the hall, and the stonehound trotted off into the distance, its solid form unwavering as it took the message across the rocky plains.

As the creatures disappeared into the horizon, Eryndal felt a brief flicker of hope. The races would know. They would be warned.

But it was only the beginning. The message had been sent. Now, they could only wait and prepare. The shadows of Raxis were growing ever closer, and the time for action was upon them.

Soren joined him on the balcony, her presence grounding him in the moment. "And now we wait."

Eryndal nodded, his eyes scanning the horizon, though his mind was already far ahead. "We wait. But we also prepare. We know what's coming. The four races are bound by the Alliance. If they come together, we might have a chance. If not…"

"We'll face the darkness alone," Roland finished, appearing at their side.

Eryndal turned from the balcony, his resolve hardening. "We won't fail. Not again."

The three of them gathered their gear, preparing to move forward. They had sent the message. The races would decide the next move. But Raxis's shadow was growing—and the time for action was rapidly approaching.

As the creatures of legend soared across Reldad, they carried more than just messages. They carried the hopes of an entire world—the hopes of four races who had once united against a common enemy, now called to rise once again before it was too late.

The Tale of the Mountains

The fire crackled softly in Kinzo Macerald's great hall, casting warm golden light across the smooth stone walls. Despite the comforting glow, a sense of unease hung in the air. Kinzo leaned forward, his sharp gnome features illuminated by the flickering flames. His eyes, keen and probing, fixed on Eryndal, Soren, and Roland, who sat silently before him. The three had gathered to hear the tale the gnome leader was about to share—a tale that carried an air of warning and possibility.

"There's something else you need to know," Kinzo began, his voice dropping into a low, deliberate tone that commanded attention. He looked to each of them in turn, his expression grave. "A story that many in the world have forgotten—or chosen to forget."

Eryndal straightened in his chair, his elven ears twitching slightly at the shift in tone. "What story?" He asked, his voice steady but tinged with curiosity.

Kinzo paused, taking a slow breath as if considering how to frame his words. "It concerns the Varnor Mountains," he said at last. "Those jagged peaks overlooking the Bershian Sea. A desolate and cursed place, if ever there was one. But the tale I speak of is not about the mountains themselves. It's about what lies within them."

The room grew still, the distant howl of wind outside the only sound. Roland leaned back in his chair, crossing his arms. "You mean the legends? Of the so-called *Judge of the Peaks*?" His tone was sceptical, but even he couldn't mask the flicker of intrigue in his eyes.

Kinzo nodded slowly. "The Judge, yes. However, the truth is far more complex than the word implies. What dwells in those mountains is ancient, older than any of our kingdoms. Some say it is a creature—a beast of immense power. Others claim it's something beyond comprehension, a force tied to the very fabric of the world. Whatever it is, the stories agree on one thing: it is alive, and it watches."

Soren frowned, her sharp features reflecting her analytical mind. "And what does it watch for? What does it want?"

Kinzo's gaze flicked to the fire as if searching for answers in its flickering flames. "No one knows," he admitted. "But the stories say it judges all who approach. Tests them. And those who fail. Well, their bones are said to litter the mountain paths."

Roland let out a low whistle, though his expression remained serious. "Sounds charming. Why bring it up now?"

Kinzo turned to him, his expression unflinching. "Because this being—whatever it is—may be the key to what you're seeking. The stories speak of its power to tip the scales of fate. To stand against darkness and bring balance to the world. If you could gain its favour."

Eryndal's breath caught. The idea was both compelling and terrifying. "But the legends say no one has ever survived seeking it out," he said quietly.

"Exactly," Kinzo replied, his tone heavy. "The mountains themselves are perilous enough. Jagged cliffs, deadly storms, creatures that hunt in the mist. But the being within. It is said to see into your very soul. It will test your strength, your resolve, your worthiness. And it does not abide failure."

The words hung in the air like a shadow, casting a pall over the room.

Legends and History of the Varnor Mountains

The Varnor Mountains were infamous across Reldad, their name spoken in hushed tones in taverns and royal halls alike. Stretching along the edge of the Bershian Sea, their jagged peaks pierced the sky like the teeth of a vast, ancient beast. For centuries, they had been the subject of countless tales—some whispered as warnings, others sung as ballads of bravery and loss.

Kinzo continued, his voice steady as he recounted what he knew. "The mountains are older than any of us can truly comprehend. Before our kingdoms rose, before the races even knew of one another, they stood as they do now. The storms that rage over the Bershian Sea are said to be born of the mountains, their winds carrying whispers of whatever dwells within."

Eryndal nodded, remembering the stories his father had shared in his youth. The Varnor Peaks were not just a natural barrier—they were alive, or so the legends claimed. The mountains themselves were said to resist intruders, shifting their paths and conjuring storms to drive away those who dared to trespass.

Roland interrupted Kinzo's thoughts with a question. "And this…*Judge*. How do the stories describe it?"

Kinzo's expression grew darker. "The descriptions vary," he said slowly. "Some say it is a beast, a great winged creature with eyes like molten gold and claws that can rend stone. Others speak of it as a shadow, formless yet immense, a presence that fills the air and chokes the breath from your lungs. Still, others say it takes on the form of your greatest fear, drawing it out of you and testing whether you can overcome it."

Soren's brow furrowed. "A shapeshifter? Or a manifestation of some kind?"

"Perhaps," Kinzo replied. "Or perhaps it's something else entirely. Something beyond our understanding. Whatever the case, it is not bound by the rules of our world. It does not live, die, or follow the laws of time. It simply *is*."

Eryndal's mind raced, piecing together fragments of what he had heard over the years. One legend, in particular, stood out—a tale of an ancient sorcerer who had ventured into the Varnor Peaks seeking ultimate power. The sorcerer had returned, but his hair had turned white, his eyes hollow and haunted. He had spoken of a presence that had tested him, and though he had survived, he had been found unworthy. He lived the rest of his days in madness, warning all who would listen never to approach the mountains.

The Judge's Role in the Balance of the World

"Why would it test those who approach?" Soren asked, her sharp mind probing for answers. "If it has such power, why not intervene directly? Why wait for others to find it?"

Kinzo considered her question carefully. "Because it is not a force of good or evil," he said at last. "It does not take sides. It is said to exist to maintain balance. It does not choose favourites or fight for glory. It waits, and it watches. It tests those who come to it, and if they prove worthy, it may grant them its power or allegiance. But if they are not." He trailed off, leaving the implication unspoken.

"Balance," Eryndal murmured, the word resonating with him. He had always been taught that the world thrived on balance—between light and darkness, chaos and order. Could this being be a manifestation of that very principle?

"Exactly," Kinzo said, catching the thread of his thought. "It is said that the Judge was created—or perhaps bound—to the mountains by forces we can't comprehend. Some say it was the gods themselves, seeking to anchor the world into stability. Others claim it was a punishment, a creature cursed to watch over the peaks for eternity. Whatever the truth, its purpose remains the same: to ensure that those who seek it are prepared for the burden they carry."

The Varnor Mountains' Mysteries

"And the mountains themselves?" Eryndal asked, his voice steady but curious. "How much of the danger is the terrain, and how much is the Judge's doing?"

Kinzo leaned back, his face thoughtful. "The mountains are treacherous in their own right. Their paths are steep and narrow, the storms fierce and unrelenting. But the stories say the Judge controls much of what happens there. The storms, the mists, the creatures that roam the peaks—they are not natural. They are its way of testing those who approach. If it does not deem you worthy, it will not allow you to reach it."

Roland shook his head. "So, it's a death trap."

"For most," Kinzo agreed. "But not for all. Those who are prepared, who are strong of will and pure of purpose, may find a path through. The question is whether you're willing to take that risk."

Eryndal's mind churned with possibilities. The Varnor Mountains were not merely a place—they were a crucible, a forge in which only the strongest could emerge whole. And the Judge, whatever it was, seemed to be the keeper of that forge.

The fire in Kinzo's hall burned low as the gnome finished his tale. The room fell silent, the weight of his words settling over the three adventurers. Though none of them spoke, a shared understanding passed between them: the Varnor Mountains were no ordinary danger. To seek out the Judge would be to step into the unknown, risking everything for a chance to tip the balance in their favour.

Chapter 8
The Journey to the Varnor Mountains

The journey to the Varnor Mountains began under the veil of an overcast dawn, the pale light casting the gnome city of Boulderstone into shades of muted grey. Eryndal, Soren, and Roland stood at the gates, their packs heavy with supplies, their thoughts weighed down by Kinzo's dire warnings. The road ahead was one of uncertainty and danger, but it was also the only path that might lead them closer to uncovering the truth about Raxis's resurgence.

The trio's route would take them through the heart of Reldad, across landscapes both wondrous and treacherous. The Wilds of the realm were as diverse as the races that called them home, and the journey would test not only their endurance but also their trust in one another.

Setting Out: The Echo of Kinzo's Words

As they departed Boulderstone, the city's bustling streets gave way to rolling hills dotted with rocky outcrops. The warmth of civilisation faded with each step, replaced by the raw presence of the wilderness.

"Kinzo wasn't exaggerating about these mountains," Roland muttered, adjusting the straps of his pack. His hand hovered near the hilt of his sword; an unconscious gesture born of caution.

Soren glanced at him, her sharp fae eyes scanning the horizon. "He wasn't just talking about the mountains. It's everything leading to them—the creatures, the weather, even the land itself. This isn't a place that welcomes travellers."

Eryndal walked a few paces ahead, his elven ears attuned to the sounds of the forest that bordered their path. He remained silent, his thoughts fixed on Kinzo's tale of the Judge. The idea of an ancient force watching, waiting, and judging gnawed at him. What would it see in him if they ever reached the peaks?

Through the Wilds of Reldad

The first leg of their journey took them through the rolling plains of Eldara, where the horizon stretched endlessly under a pale blue sky. Though the land seemed serene, it held a tension, a sense of being watched by unseen eyes.

At night, they camped under the open sky, the stars above a reminder of the vastness of the world and the trials yet to come. The fire crackled as Soren traced patterns in the dirt with a stick, her expression contemplative.

"It feels like the land itself is holding its breath," she murmured, her voice soft.

Roland, leaning back against his pack, glanced at her. "You're not wrong. The closer we get to those mountains, the heavier it feels. Like we're walking into the belly of something alive."

Encounters Along the Path

The journey wasn't without its moments of respite and intrigue. Along the way, they encountered individuals from the far-flung corners of Reldad—members of the four races who lived far from the centres of power yet carried with them the wisdom and resilience of their kin.

1. The Faes of Luminara

Deep in the bioluminescent forests of Luminara, the trio stumbled upon a gathering of faes. These ethereal beings, their glowing forms like will-o'-the-wisps, greeted Soren with a melodic hum in their Ancient Tongue. The faes shared supplies and stories, speaking of strange occurrences: shadows moving in places where no light should falter, whispers carried on the wind that seemed to beckon travellers towards danger.

"The world feels…unstable," one of the faes said, her luminous eyes reflecting a deep sadness. "Raxis's shadow grows longer each day, though few realise it. We hear it in the songs of the forest, in the way the light dims where it once shone brightly."

Soren thanked them in her melodic tongue, their conversation a harmonious blend of sound and meaning. As the group departed, the faes' warnings lingered in their minds like a faint, haunting melody.

2. The Elves of Eldara

Later, the trio crossed paths with an elven patrol guarding a sacred grove nestled within the rolling hills of Eldara. These elves, tall and graceful, regarded the travellers with a mixture of suspicion and curiosity.

Eryndal stepped forward, bowing his head slightly as he greeted them in flawless Elvish. The words rolled off his tongue like a melody, surprising both Roland and Soren, who had rarely heard him speak of his heritage.

The elves' leader, a stoic warrior named Vaelith, studied Eryndal with narrowed eyes before nodding in approval. "You carry the grace of our kin," he said, his tone measured. "Few who wander these lands remember the Old Tongue, let alone speak it with such precision."

The patrol offered the group healing salves and guidance, warning them of the treacherous paths ahead. "The Varnor Mountains are a place of endings,"

Vaelith said gravely. "Few who go there return, and those who do are never the same."

A Conversation Beneath the Stars

That evening, as they camped under a canopy of stars, Roland approached Eryndal. The firelight cast flickering shadows across his face, softening the lines of his typically hardened expression.

"Your Elvish is perfect," Roland said, breaking the silence. "Almost too perfect."

Eryndal glanced up from where he was securing his pack, a flicker of surprise crossing his features. "My father taught me," he replied simply.

Roland's expression softened further, a note of familiarity in his voice. "I knew him, you know. Many years ago, before…" He trailed off, the weight of unspoken memories hanging between them.

"You knew him?" Eryndal's voice held a mixture of curiosity and apprehension.

Roland nodded. "He was a good man. Brave, sharp as a blade. But he had secrets. Things he didn't share, even with those closest to him."

Eryndal looked into the fire, his brow furrowed. "He spoke in riddles sometimes. Especially near the end. About sacrifices and a great danger rising. But he never told me what he meant."

Roland placed a firm hand on Eryndal's shoulder, his grip both reassuring and grounding. "Whatever those secrets were, they shaped him. And they've shaped you, whether you realise it or not. You carry more of him than you think. And I believe he knew you'd have to face this darkness one day."

Eryndal nodded slowly, his resolve hardening. "Then I'll make sure I'm ready."

The Growing Weight of the Mountains

As the days turned into weeks, the trio pressed onward. The Varnor Mountains began to loom on the horizon, their jagged peaks shrouded in perpetual mist. The closer they came, the more oppressive the air grew. It was as if the mountains themselves were aware of their presence, their shadow stretching far beyond the physical.

Each night, the howling winds carried whispers that seemed to speak directly to their fears and doubts. Soren, usually so composed, found herself glancing over her shoulder more often. Roland grew more guarded, his sword never far from his hand. Even Eryndal, whose calm demeanour rarely wavered, felt the weight of an unseen force pressing against his mind.

"The mountains are testing us already," Soren remarked one evening, her voice barely audible over the crackling fire. "They don't want us to come closer."

Roland snorted, though his tone lacked its usual confidence. "Then they'd better get used to disappointment."

The Land's Final Warning

On the final stretch before reaching the foothills of the Varnor Mountains, the group encountered one last obstacle: a dense, twisting forest where the trees seemed to shift and sway of their own accord. The air was thick with tension, every sound amplified as if the forest itself was alive.

Eryndal led the way, his sharp eyes catching glimpses of movement in the shadows. At one point, a low growl echoed through the underbrush, sending a chill down their spines.

"We're being watched," Roland muttered, his hand on his sword hilt.

"We've been watched for days," Soren replied, her tone resigned but firm.

When they finally emerged from the forest, the sight that greeted them was both awe-inspiring and foreboding: the Varnor Mountains in their full, terrible majesty. The peaks rose like jagged spears, their tips lost in swirling clouds. Lightning flickered within the mist, casting a fleeting, eerie glow over the dark stone.

For a long moment, none of them spoke. The mountains seemed to hum with an ancient, implacable power as if daring them to come closer.

"This is it," Eryndal said at last, his voice steady despite the weight of what lay ahead.

The others nodded; their expressions grim but resolute. The journey to the Varnor Mountains had tested their mettle, but it was clear that the true trials were only just beginning.

The Ambush in the Ravine

The Varnor Mountains loomed closer with each step, their jagged peaks obscured by thick, swirling clouds. The path to the mountains was treacherous, narrowing into a steep ravine flanked by towering cliffs. The wind howled through the crags, carrying with it an unnatural chill that prickled at the group's nerves. Soren moved with quiet vigilance, her keen fae senses alert to every shift in the air, while Eryndal led cautiously, his elven eyes scanning the rocky terrain for signs of movement. Roland, ever the seasoned warrior, brought up the rear, his hand never far from the hilt of his sword.

The ravine seemed designed to ensnare. Its rocky walls towered high above, jagged and oppressive, the narrow passage creating a sense of entrapment. The trio's footsteps echoed eerily off the stone; a sound swallowed almost immediately by the moaning wind.

They had just reached the centre of the ravine when the ambush began.

The Attackers Strike

From the cliffs above, shadowy figures emerged as if birthed from the rock itself—dozens of them, garbed in dark robes marked with sigils that glowed faintly in the dim light.

Their weapons, jagged and pulsing with malevolent energy, reflected the dark magic that had corrupted their souls.

"Above us!" Soren shouted, her voice cutting through the rising chaos.

Arrows rained down first, black-fletched and barbed with serrated tips. Eryndal moved with the speed of his kind, his blades flashing as he parried the deadly projectiles with a precision that left Roland momentarily awed. Soren raised her hands, summoning a shimmer of protective magic that deflected several arrows before they could reach Roland or herself.

And then the attackers descended. With inhuman agility, they leapt from the cliffs, landing in the narrow path with deadly intent. Their movements were fluid and unnatural, as though driven by something other than their own will.

The Beast Emerges

The cacophony of clashing steel, magic, and snarled commands was broken by a bone-chilling growl that seemed to reverberate through the very stone. Emerging from the shadows was a hulking figure—half-man, half-beast—with matted fur as black as night and eyes that burned crimson. Its claws gleamed like obsidian, unnaturally sharp, and its presence sent a wave of dread through the air.

Roland froze as his gaze fell upon the creature, his breath catching in his throat.

The werewolf's snarl deepened as it locked eyes with Roland. The beast didn't hesitate, lunging forward with a speed that defied its massive frame.

The Battle Unfolds

Eryndal met the charge first, his elven-like agility allowing him to dodge the creature's initial swipe. His twin blades flashed in a flurry of strikes aimed at the beast's exposed flank. But the werewolf's hide was tougher than it appeared—Eryndal's swords glanced off the fur as though it were reinforced steel. With a snarl, the beast lashed out, its claws raking across Eryndal's side.

Eryndal staggered, his face pale as blood seeped from the deep wounds. There was something unnatural about the injury—dark tendrils of magic seemed to writhe within the gashes, corrupting the flesh.

"Eryndal!" Soren cried; her voice filled with alarm. She extended her hands, unleashing a burst of fae magic that disoriented the creature, buying Eryndal enough time to stagger back.

Roland's attention snapped to the werewolf. The sight of the beast awakened memories he had buried deep, memories of a night drenched in blood and grief.

"You," Roland growled, his voice trembling with rage. He pointed his sword at the werewolf. "I know you. I'll never forget the monster that killed my son!"

A Haunted Past

The werewolf paused, its glowing red eyes narrowing as if recognising Roland in turn. For a moment, the chaos around them seemed to still. The wind howled through the ravine, carrying with it the ghostly echoes of Roland's anguished cries from that fateful night years ago.

Roland's mind was flooded with memories. He saw his son, barely old enough to wield a blade but full of promise, lying lifeless in his arms. He remembered the beast's blood-streaked maw, its crimson eyes filled with merciless hunger as it tore his world apart.

"You took everything from me!" Roland roared, his voice breaking as he charged the beast.

Roland vs. the Werewolf

The werewolf met Roland's charge head-on, its claws clashing against the seasoned warrior's blade. The force of the impact sent a shockwave through the narrow ravine, causing loose rocks to tumble from the cliffs above. Roland's strikes were fierce and unrelenting, driven by years of pent-up fury and grief.

The werewolf, however, was no ordinary foe. It moved with a predator's grace, dodging and countering Roland's attacks with brutal efficiency. Its claws struck like thunder, each swipe narrowly missing the warrior as he twisted and ducked.

Despite his skill, Roland was pushed to his limits. The beast was faster, stronger, and fuelled by dark magic. Every swing of his sword felt heavier; every breath was harder to catch.

Soren, seeing Roland falter, leapt into action. With a flick of her wrist, she cast an enchantment that momentarily froze the werewolf in place, its limbs locking as if bound by invisible chains.

"Now, Roland!" she shouted.

A Fatal Blow

Seizing the opportunity, Roland surged forward. His blade, glowing faintly with an enchantment gifted by the elves, plunged into the werewolf's chest. The beast let out a deafening roar, its claws thrashing wildly as it tried to break free. Roland twisted the blade with all his strength, driving it deeper until the werewolf's movements slowed and finally ceased.

The creature's crimson eyes dimmed, and its body began to dissolve into ash, carried away by the howling wind.

Roland stood over the pile of ash, his chest heaving, his sword trembling in his hand. For a moment, he felt a flicker of triumph, but it was quickly replaced by the hollow ache of loss. Killing the beast hadn't brought his son back.

The Aftermath

The battle wasn't without cost. Eryndal lay unconscious, his wounds festering with dark corruption. Soren knelt by his side, her hands glowing with fae magic as she tried to stem the spread of the malevolent energy.

"Stay with me, Eryndal," she whispered, her voice uncharacteristically soft.

Roland knelt beside them, his face pale and lined with exhaustion. "Will he make it?" He asked, his voice hoarse.

Soren's expression was grim. "I don't know. The magic in those claws…it's unlike anything I've seen before."

Roland's gaze drifted back to the pile of ash, his jaw tightening. The werewolf was gone, but its legacy remained—a reminder that some wounds never truly healed. As the wind howled through the ravine, carrying the echoes of the battle into the distance, Roland silently vowed that he would do whatever it took to ensure his comrades didn't suffer the same loss he had.

A New Ally

The dust of the battle lingered in the air, thick and suffocating, as the ravine fell silent. The lifeless bodies of Raxis's followers lay scattered amidst the jagged rocks, their black robes torn and bloodied. Eryndal's limp form was the centre of Soren's frantic attention, his pale face streaked with sweat and his breathing shallow. Roland stood over them both, his sword still drawn, his eyes scanning the cliffs above for any lingering threat.

The oppressive silence of the aftermath was shattered by a low hum—a sound that seemed to rise not from the earth, but from the very air around them. The wind shifted, carrying with it an eerie warmth that pricked their skin. From the shadows beyond the ravine came a glow—soft and faint at first, then growing brighter, until a figure emerged, cloaked in shimmering light.

At first, the figure seemed humanoid, its form delicate and ethereal, but even as they watched, it shifted. The light condensed and stretched, becoming an eagle with wings ablaze like the morning sun. Then it morphed into a glimmer fox, its glowing eyes piercing and sharp, before flowing again into the shape of a mighty stonehound with a mane of golden fire and then an elegant and strong stag. The group froze, awestruck and wary, as the being finally settled into a humanoid form once more—a figure of translucent brilliance, its outline flickering like a flame caught in the wind.

Its voice echoed not from its mouth, but directly into their minds, resonating like the chime of crystal bells. "I am Emberthane," it said, each word carrying a weight that seemed to press against their souls. "I am the guardian of these lands, bound to this realm for centuries. I have watched your journey from afar, drawn by your courage...and your despair."

Emberthane's Origins and Purpose

Soren's grip tightened on her staff as she stepped forward, her fae instincts warring with her curiosity. "A guardian?" She echoed, her voice both cautious and intrigued. "Of what?"

Emberthane's form flickered again, its face turning towards the jagged peaks of the Varnor Mountains. "Of this land," it replied. "Of its magic, its secrets, and its burdens. Long ago, when the four races were first formed, the ancient mages created guardians to ensure a balance between the light and the dark. I am one of those guardians."

The being gestured to the amulet hanging from its neck. It was a radiant fragment of crystal, pulsing faintly with light. "This is one of four fragments—pieces of a greater whole forged in the fires of the Starforge. Together, the four fragments form the Amulet of Equinox, a relic of unimaginable power designed to hold back the forces of chaos. My fragment is bound to me, just as the others are bound to my kin across the realms."

Roland's eyes narrowed as he studied the glowing figure. "And what do you want with us?" He asked, his voice low and edged with suspicion.

Emberthane's gaze turned to Eryndal, who lay unconscious and pale, his wounds blackened and festering with dark magic. "I do not seek you," the guardian replied. "But the darkness you face has seeped into this land, threatening all that I protect. Your struggle has stirred the balance, and now I must act."

The being knelt beside Eryndal, its translucent hand hovering over his chest. "He is gravely wounded. The dark magic that burns within him is ancient and insidious. It seeks to consume him entirely."

Soren dropped to her knees beside Eryndal, her eyes wide with desperation. "Can you save him?" She asked, her voice trembling.

Emberthane's form shifted again, flowing into the shape of a glimmer fox. It lowered its head, its glowing eyes locking onto Soren's. "I can," it said, its voice now a low growl that resonated through the ravine. "But the price will be steep. This magic cannot be wielded without consequence."

The Price of the Amulet's Power

Roland stepped forward, his jaw set and his sword still clutched in his hand. "What kind of consequence?" He demanded, his voice a mixture of fear and determination. "His life is worth any cost."

The glimmer fox's form dissolved into a luminous stag, its antlers sparkling with frost-like light. "The price is not death," it said. "But a burden. The power of the fragment will heal him, but it will also bind him to me—to this land and its magic. He will carry its weight for the rest of his days, just as I have. It will change him in ways even I cannot foresee."

Roland's hand tightened on the hilt of his sword. "He's already burdened with enough," he muttered.

Soren looked up, her violet eyes glistening with unshed tears. "We don't have a choice," she said firmly. "If we don't save him, he'll die."

The stag nodded solemnly and lowered its head, the amulet around its neck beginning to glow brighter. "Then it shall be done."

The Healing Ritual

Emberthane's form became more solid as it placed the amulet directly onto Eryndal's chest. The crystal pulsed with a light that grew stronger with each beat, spreading across his body like liquid fire. Eryndal's body convulsed, his back arching as the dark magic within him fought against the healing power of the fragment.

The group watched in tense silence as the light grew blinding, forcing them to shield their eyes. Emberthane's voice echoed through the ravine, its tone commanding and resolute. "Darkness, be gone! Your hold on this soul is broken!"

Eryndal gasped, his body shuddering violently before collapsing back to the ground. The light dimmed, and for a moment, all was still.

When Eryndal's eyes finally fluttered open, they glowed faintly with the same light that emanated from Emberthane. His wounds had closed, leaving behind faint, jagged scars that seemed to shimmer faintly in the dim light.

"What...what happened?" He asked weakly, his voice hoarse.

"You have been saved," Emberthane said, now appearing once more in its humanoid form. "But you are no longer the same. The fragment's magic has touched you, and you are now bound to its power. It will guide you in your struggle, but it will also demand much of you in return."

Revealing Emberthane's Watchful Eye

Roland sheathed his sword, his eyes narrowing as he stepped closer to the glowing figure. "You said you've been watching us. For how long?"

Emberthane tilted its head, its translucent form flickering. "Since you first entered my domain," it replied. "I am the guardian of these lands. I see all who tread within them."

Soren frowned. "If you've been watching us, why didn't you help us sooner? Why let us fight alone?"

Emberthane's gaze softened, and it shifted into the form of an eagle. "Because this is not my fight," it said. "I am bound to protect the balance of this realm, not to intervene in the struggles of mortals. But your battle has disrupted that balance. The darkness you face threatens not only you but all that I am sworn to protect."

Roland's expression darkened. "So, you waited until it was convenient for you," he said bitterly.

The eagle's form dissolved into that of a stonehound, its glowing mane bristling with energy. "Do not mistake caution for indifference," it said, its voice a low rumble. "I act not for convenience, but for necessity. Your struggle has forced my hand."

The Amulet and Its Purpose

Soren's gaze lingered on the amulet around Emberthane's neck. "You said there are four fragments," she said. "Where are the others?"

Emberthane's form shimmered as it spoke. "The fragments were scattered long ago, hidden across the realms to prevent their power from being used for destruction. Each is guarded by one of my kin, bound to their land just as I am to mine. Together, they form the Amulet of Equinox, a relic capable of endless power. But apart, their power is limited."

Eryndal, still weak but alert, struggled to sit up. "So, if we find the others, we could use them against Raxis?"

Emberthane nodded. "Perhaps. But the fragments are not tools to be wielded lightly. Their power comes at a cost, as you have already seen. To claim them is to accept their burden."

A New Ally, a New Hope

The cold night air clung to the group as they made camp in the foothills of the Varnor Mountains. The echoes of their recent battle still reverberated in their minds—screams, the clash of steel, and the unearthly growl of the werewolf that had nearly killed Eryndal. Though the immediate threat had passed, tension lingered in the air like smoke.

Eryndal lay on a makeshift bedroll, his breathing steady but shallow. His face was pale, though a faint light now glimmered in his eyes—a remnant of the magic that had saved his life. Nearby, Soren tended to him, her hands deftly applying salves to his wounds. The potions they carried could only do so much; it was Emberthane's intervention that had turned the tide.

Roland sat apart from them; his broad frame silhouetted against the crackling fire. His sword lay across his knees, the blade reflecting the flickering flames. He was silent, his gaze fixed on the flames as if searching for answers within them. The faint glow of Emberthane's form, now settled in its luminous glimmer fox shape, illuminated the edges of the camp.

It was Roland who broke the silence, his voice low and rough. "That creature," he began, his tone more bitter than weary, "the one that attacked you." He paused, tightening his grip on the sword. "It wasn't just any of Raxis's beasts. It was the same one that killed my son."

The words hung in the air like a physical weight.

Revealing the Past

Eryndal turned his head weakly towards Roland, his brow furrowing as he processed the revelation. "Your son?" He asked, his voice hoarse but steady.

Roland nodded, his jaw tightening. "Years ago," he said, his voice heavy with grief, "during the Battle of the Broken Crown. I was a soldier, a commander. My son, Alric, was young—too young to fight, but he begged to join the war effort. Said he couldn't sit idle while his father fought for the realm." He exhaled deeply, his eyes hardening. "I should have said no. But I didn't."

He paused; his gaze distant as if he could see the memory playing out before him. "That battle. It was chaos. We were holding the line against Raxis's forces, but their numbers were overwhelming. Then that thing appeared." His voice grew harsher, laced with rage. "A werewolf. But not like the others. This one was larger, faster and stronger. Its eyes burned red, and its claws could cut through steel. It tore through our ranks like we were nothing."

Roland's hands trembled as he gripped his sword. "I saw it coming for Alric. I tried to reach him, but I was too far. It…" He swallowed hard, his voice breaking for the first time. "It killed him. Right in front of me. I managed to strike it down, or so I thought. But somehow, it survived."

Soren looked up from her work, her violet eyes wide with a mix of shock and sorrow. "And now it's here again," she murmured.

Roland nodded; his expression grim. "I thought I'd buried it with Alric. But it seems Raxis's darkness has a way of keeping its monsters alive."

Eryndal, despite his exhaustion, pushed himself up slightly, placing a hand on Roland's shoulder. "We'll finish it," he said, his voice filled with quiet resolve. "Together."

The Gathering Storm

Soren sat back, her hands stilling as she considered their situation. "That creature wasn't here by coincidence," she said. "Raxis's followers were after something, and I don't think it was just us."

Her gaze shifted to Emberthane, who stood at the edge of the firelight, its glowing glimmer fox form observing them silently. "You know why they're here, don't you?" She asked.

Emberthane stepped closer, its luminous form casting faint shadows across the rocky terrain. "Yes," it said, its voice resonating softly in their minds. "The amulet I wear contains more than healing magic. It is a key, a fragment of a power long thought lost. If Morva Sable seeks to resurrect Raxis, this amulet may be part of her plan."

The revelation struck them like a thunderclap.

Roland rose to his feet, his expression darkening. "What do you mean?" He demanded.

Emberthane shifted into the form of a stag, its antlers shimmering like frost in the moonlight. "This amulet is one of four," it explained. "Each tied to the elements of this world—fire, water, earth, and air. Together, they form the Amulet of Equinox, a relic forged to maintain balance in the realm. It was created in a time when the darkness threatened to consume everything, and its power was used to banish Raxis to the void."

Soren's eyes narrowed, her mind racing. "So, if Morva Sable gathers all four fragments…"

"She could summon a force strong enough to bring Raxis back in full power," Emberthane finished. "I have kept this fragment hidden for centuries, but its light drew her followers to these mountains. She knows it exists."

A Dangerous Mission

Roland's hand tightened around the hilt of his sword. "Then we keep it from her at all costs," he said firmly.

Eryndal nodded, his strength slowly returning. "And we find the other three," he added. "If she can use them, then so can we."

Soren hesitated; her mind clouded with doubt. "Do we even know where the other fragments are?" She asked. "Or what they're capable of?"

Emberthane's form flickered, shifting into a glowing eagle that perched on a nearby rock. "The fragments were scattered long ago to prevent their power from being abused," it said. "Each is guarded by a being like myself, bound to its land and its magic. Their locations are hidden, known only to those who are deemed worthy."

"And how do we prove ourselves worthy?" Roland asked, his tone laced with scepticism.

Emberthane's gaze bore into him, its glowing eyes unyielding. "By facing the trials ahead. The path will not be easy, nor will it be clear. But the magic that binds this amulet now flows through Eryndal. He will feel its presence and guide you to what lies beyond."

All eyes turned to Eryndal, who looked down at the faintly glowing scars on his chest. "I don't feel anything," he said quietly.

"You will," Emberthane replied. "In time. The magic is still settling within you. But when the moment comes, you will know."

Strength in Unity

The group fell silent, the weight of their mission pressing down on them like the very mountains around them. Soren was the first to speak, her voice soft but steady. "We've already come this far. We've faced Raxis's followers and survived. If we can do that, we can find the other fragments."

Roland nodded, his expression hard but resolute. "We don't have a choice. If Morva Sable succeeds, the whole realm will fall. We will stop her, no matter the cost."

Eryndal looked at each of them in turn, his gaze lingering on Roland. "This isn't just about stopping her," he said. "It's about setting things right. For your son. For everyone who Raxis has taken from us."

Roland's jaw tightened, and he gave a curt nod.

Emberthane stepped back, its luminous form glowing faintly against the darkness. "You have strength," it said. "And you have hope. Together, those may be enough to face what lies ahead."

A New Dawn

As the first light of dawn broke over the peaks, the group began to pack their gear, their movements slow but determined. Emberthane stood silently at the edge of the camp, its luminous form casting faint shadows against the rocks. The guardian, now fully committed to their cause, had taken on the shape of a glowing stag with antlers that sparkled like frost.

Soren turned to the shimmering figure. "Will you come with us?" She asked, her voice filled with both hope and caution.

Emberthane inclined its head. "I will guide you," it said. "The mountains are my domain, and their paths are treacherous even for the strong of heart. There are dangers here that even Raxis's followers dare not disturb. But together, we may find a way through."

Roland gave a nod, his expression hard but resolute. "We'll follow your lead, but we can't afford to waste time. If Morva Sable is hunting the other fragments, every moment counts."

Eryndal, still recovering but bolstered by the magic now coursing through him, gave a faint smile. "At least we won't be stumbling blind anymore."

Emberthane shifted into the form of a luminous glimmer fox, its glowing eyes scanning the rugged terrain ahead. "Stay close," it said. "The path is not what it seems, and the mountains will test you in ways you cannot yet imagine."

With the guardian leading the way, the group pressed onward, climbing steadily into the jagged heights of the Varnor Mountains. The air grew colder, and the landscape became increasingly desolate, but Emberthane's radiant presence served as a beacon of hope.

Though the journey was far from over, they no longer felt entirely alone. They had gained an ally not only in their battle against Raxis but also in navigating the harsh, unforgiving wilderness ahead. With Emberthane at their side, the path through the mountains—and to the fragments of the Amulet of Equinox—seemed just a little less impossible.

Their journey continued, the peaks looming higher with every step, as the faint glow of their new ally lit the way forward.

Chapter 9
The Four Amulets

The wind cut through the jagged peaks of the Varnor Mountains like a blade, carrying with it a biting chill that sank into the bones. The group pressed onward, their breaths coming in white plumes, their muscles weary from the climb. Yet the presence of Emberthane, shifting between forms—a luminous glimmer fox, an elegant stag, a mighty stonehound, a blazing eagle and a shimmering humanoid figure—gave them purpose and direction. Its glow cut through the murk of the mountain paths, a beacon of hope in the desolate wilderness.

But as they followed their strange, otherworldly guide, Emberthane's voice resonated in their minds, weaving a tale that held the weight of ages. It spoke not just of the mountains or the dangers ahead, but of the four amulets—artefacts that would shape the course of their journey and the fate of the world.

The Tale of the Amulets

"Long before the Alliance of the Heart," Emberthane began, its voice carrying a solemn reverence, "this world was untamed. Magic flowed freely, wild and pure, shaping the land and all who dwelt within it. It was a time of creation and chaos, where the elements roamed unchecked, and no mortal had yet dreamed of dominion over them."

The group paused to catch their breath as Emberthane's words filled the air, the tale demanding their full attention.

"In those days," it continued, its form shifting into a glowing eagle perched on a nearby rock, "a cabal of ancient sorcerers sought to harness this primal force. They were not content to live in harmony with the world; they wished to command it, to bend its will to their own. In their arrogance, they forged the four amulets—each imbued with the essence of a single element: earth, air, fire, and water. The sorcerers believed that by combining the amulets, they could transcend mortality and wield the power of gods."

Soren's sharp gaze met Emberthane's glowing eyes. "Let me guess," she said dryly. "It didn't go as planned."

Emberthane shifted into its humanoid form, its expression unreadable. "Indeed, it did not. The sorcerers underestimated the forces they sought to control. The amulets, while incredibly powerful, were not forged with the natural balance of magic in mind. Instead, they were bound by a darker, more ancient force—one born of ambition and greed. That force corrupted the amulets, twisting their power and the sorcerers themselves."

Roland's hand tightened on the hilt of his sword. "What happened to them?"

"They turned on one another," Emberthane said. "Each sorcerer sought to claim the amulets for themselves, believing they could harness their full potential alone. Their war tore the land apart, leaving scars that remain even now. Rivers boiled, mountains crumbled, and forests turned to ash. In the end, none of them succeeded. Their ambitions consumed them, leaving their creations behind as relics of their failure."

Why the Amulets Were Not Destroyed

Eryndal frowned, his steps slowing as he absorbed the tale. "If the amulets were so dangerous, why weren't they destroyed?"

"They could not be destroyed," Emberthane replied, its voice heavy with the weight of ages. "The magic within them is too powerful, too deeply intertwined with the essence of this world. Attempts to destroy them only unleashed their wrath upon the land. The most the ancients could do was hide them, scattering them across the farthest reaches of the world, where no one would dare to seek them."

Roland grunted, his brow furrowing. "Yet here we are, seeking them."

"Not by choice," Soren muttered.

"The amulets were hidden in places tied to their essence," Emberthane continued, ignoring the interruption. "The Amulet of Earth was buried deep beneath a mountain, in a labyrinth of stone and shadow, this is what I carry. The Amulet of Air was locked within a storm that never ceases, beneath the waves of Sirrath. The Amulet of Fire rests within the heart of a volcanic chasm, its flames eternal, hidden amongst a desert. And the Amulet of Water lies within the abyss of an endless sea, its depths guarded by ancient creatures and the murky Blackwater Marshes."

Eryndal's eyes widened as the enormity of the task began to sink in. "And the amulet you carry?"

Emberthane shifted into the form of a glowing wolf, its luminous eyes locking onto Eryndal. Around its neck, the Amulet of Earth pulsed faintly with light. "This is the first. It was entrusted to me long ago, to keep it safe from those who would abuse its power. But its light has grown stronger of late, a sign that the balance is shifting. Morva Sable seeks the others, and if she succeeds…"

It did not finish the thought. It did not need to.

The Amulets' Importance

As they neared a narrow ledge overlooking a deep ravine, Soren turned to Emberthane. "If Morva Sable gets her hands on all four amulets, what happens?"

"The consequences would be catastrophic," Emberthane said. "The amulets, when united, can awaken a power capable of reshaping the world. That is what the sorcerers sought, and what Morva Sable now seeks. But such power cannot be controlled. It will consume her, as it consumed them, and leave only destruction in its wake."

Eryndal's jaw tightened. "Then we can't let her succeed."

"Agreed," Emberthane said. "But the amulets can also be used to restore balance. If wielded by those with pure intent, they can heal the wounds left by the sorcerers' war. That is why they must not fall into the wrong hands."

Roland's voice was grim as he spoke, "Then we need to find the others before she does. Whatever it takes."

The Weight of Responsibility

As the group continued their climb, Emberthane's words lingered in their minds, a heavy reminder of the stakes they faced. The tale of the amulets was not just a story—it was a warning, a glimpse into the darkness that had consumed the past and now threatened the present.

Each step they took brought them closer to the unknown, the weight of their task growing heavier with every mile. But with Emberthane at their side, they carried not just the burden of responsibility, but also the spark of hope—a fragile, flickering light against the encroaching shadow.

And so, with the tale of the four amulets etched into their hearts, they pressed on into the mountains, their resolve stronger than ever.

The group paused on the narrow ledge, the wind howling like a living thing. Below them yawned a deep chasm, its bottom lost to the shadows of the late afternoon. Emberthane's light glowed softly in the growing dimness, illuminating their weary faces. As its form shimmered and shifted into a human-like figure, its translucent eyes fixed on them, the being seemed almost more memory than substance.

For a moment, there was only the sound of the wind and the faint hum of Emberthane's magic. Then it spoke, its voice low and solemn, resonating as if it carried the weight of countless centuries.

"I was not always the guardian you see before you," it began. "Long ago, I was flesh and blood, a mortal like you. I lived in these mountains, sworn to protect my people and the magic of this land."

A Protector's Duty

The wind surged, and the group huddled closer, listening intently. Emberthane's gaze seemed to drift into the distance, as though seeing a world long vanished.

"My name," it said softly, "has been forgotten, even by me. But in those days, I was known as a protector, a warrior trained in both blade and magic. The Varnor Mountains were my home, a place of harsh beauty and great danger. My people relied on me to defend them against the beasts that roamed these peaks and the darker forces that sought to claim their lives and souls."

Eryndal leaned on his staff, his curiosity evident despite his exhaustion. "What forces?" He asked.

Emberthane's form shimmered slightly, its edges blurring as it answered. "During the Wars of Old, the mountains were a battleground for the sorcerers who created the amulets. Their thirst for power spilt into every corner of the land, corrupting even the wild places. As their war raged, the magic they unleashed seeped into the earth, the rivers, the skies. The mountains themselves bore the scars of their conflict— crumbling peaks, valleys where no life could grow. And when the war ended, the remnants of their power were left behind, scattered and dangerous."

Discovering the Amulet

Roland's voice cut through the chill air; his tone sharp with purpose. "And the amulet? How did you find it?"

Emberthane inclined its head, its glowing eyes locking onto Roland's. "It was not by accident, though at the time, it felt like fate had led me to it. I had been tracking a band of raiders who had begun terrorising my people, stealing their food and destroying their homes. I followed them into the heart of the mountains, where few dared to tread. The path was treacherous, the air thin, the danger immense."

It shifted, taking the shape of a glimmer fox, pacing along the ledge as if reliving the memory.

"I pursued them to a hidden cavern; one I had never seen before despite my years in these mountains. The cavern was vast, its walls lined with strange crystals that glowed faintly, as though alive. At its centre was a pedestal of carved stone, and upon it rested the Amulet of Earth. Its light was dim, but its presence was undeniable. I could feel its power, like a heartbeat in the air."

Soren stepped forward, her eyes narrowing as she spoke, "And the raiders? Did they try to take it?"

"They did not understand what they had found," Emberthane replied. "To them, it was just another artefact, something to plunder and sell. But as they approached the pedestal, the amulet's magic awoke. The earth itself rose against them—stalagmites erupting from the ground, walls collapsing, the air filled with the sound of grinding stone. It was as if the mountain were alive, protecting its treasure."

The Price of Protection

Emberthane paused, its glimmer fox form dissolving into its humanoid shape. It stood motionless, its glowing eyes haunted. "I could have turned back then," it said softly. "I could have left the amulet where it was, hidden and guarded by the mountain's wrath. But I knew that as long as it remained there, others would come. The raiders were just the first. If they had survived long enough to speak of it, the amulet's location would become known. And then...there would be no end to the bloodshed."

The group exchanged uneasy glances. Eryndal's voice was low when he asked, "So you took it?"

"I had no choice," Emberthane said, its voice filled with quiet resignation. "I stepped forward, past the bodies of the raiders, and claimed the amulet. The moment I touched it; I felt its power surge through me. It was overwhelming—a torrent of strength and knowledge, but also pain. The amulet was bound to the earth, to the mountain itself, and by taking it, I became bound as well."

The being's translucent hand drifted to the glowing amulet around its neck, the light pulsing faintly with its words. "It changed me. My body, my soul—they were no longer mine. I became something else. A part of the mountain, a part of the land. My mortal life was gone, replaced by this existence. I became its guardian, its keeper, charged with ensuring that it never fell into the wrong hands."

The Weight of Immortality

The fire in Roland's eyes dimmed slightly as he asked, "And you've been like this ever since?"

"Yes," Emberthane replied. "For centuries, I have watched over the amulet, hidden in the mountains, my existence tied to its power. At first, I thought I had made the right choice. My people were safe, the amulet secure. But as the years passed, I realised the cost of my decision. I was no longer part of the world I had fought to protect. I became a shadow, a memory, watching as time swept my people away. Their faces, their names—all lost to history."

Its voice grew softer, tinged with sorrow. "Even now, I cannot tell you if my sacrifice was worth it. I have spent lifetimes guarding this amulet, ensuring that it did not fall into the hands of those who would misuse it. And yet, here we are. The world is once again in peril, and the amulets are no longer safe in hiding. Perhaps they never were."

Soren's expression softened; her sharp tongue held in check for once. "You did what you had to," she said. "If you hadn't taken the amulet, someone else would have, and who knows what they would have done with it."

The Call to Action

Emberthane turned to face the group fully, its form glowing brighter. "Perhaps," it said. "But the time for regret is over. The amulet must be used—not to conquer, but to protect. Its power, and that of the other three, must be harnessed to stop Morva Sable and the darkness she seeks to unleash."

Eryndal stepped forward, his expression resolute despite the lingering pain of his wounds. "And we'll help you do it. We'll find the other amulets and ensure they don't fall into her hands."

Emberthane inclined its head. "The path will be dangerous, and the cost high. But if you are willing, then we stand a chance."

The group nodded; their determination renewed. As they resumed their climb, Emberthane's tale lingered in their minds—a reminder of the sacrifices already made and the challenges yet to come. The Amulet of Earth, once a dormant artefact buried in the heart of the mountains, was now a symbol of hope and a call to action.

And as the wind howled around them, carrying the echoes of Emberthane's ancient resolve, they knew there was no turning back.

The Locations of the Remaining Amulets

The companions continued their ascent into the Varnor Mountains, the weight of Emberthane's tale pressing heavily upon them. Though the sky was clear, the chill of the high peaks seemed deeper now, as though the story of the amulets had drawn the very cold of the void closer. Each step carried the group higher and further into uncertainty, and each word from Emberthane added another layer of peril to the journey ahead.

The Amulet of Water: Reldad's Shadow

"One of the amulets," Emberthane began, its voice as steady as the crunch of boots on snow, "is already lost to us. The Amulet of Water rests in the hands of Raxis's followers, its power corrupting the Blackwater Marshes."

Roland scowled, his fingers tightening on the hilt of his sword. "How long have they had it?"

"Years," Emberthane replied grimly, its form flickering briefly as though the thought pained it. "Though the marshes have always been a place of decay, their descent into unholy ruin began not long ago. Travellers speak of the marshes shifting, of stagnant waters rising as if alive, drowning villages in their path. Some say the dead walk there, pulled from their watery graves to serve a new master."

Soren's gaze sharpened, her lips tightening. "Then why hasn't the Alliance taken action? Surely they know the amulet is there."

"They do," Emberthane said. "But the marshes are vast and treacherous. Even the Alliance fears what they cannot fully comprehend. Besides, to strike against Raxis's followers in their stronghold would require strength the Alliance no longer possesses."

Eryndal's voice was quiet but firm. "And the power of the Amulet of Water only strengthens them further."

Emberthane nodded. "Indeed. Its influence flows through the marshes, its energy warping the land and the creatures within. The amulet's presence is why Raxis's followers chose the marshes as their foothold. They draw strength from its dark tides."

Roland's jaw clenched, his eyes burning with determination. "Then we'll take it back. I don't care what dangers lie within those swamps. That amulet doesn't belong in their hands."

"Patience, Roland," Soren said, her tone measured. "First, we need to ensure the others are secure. The Amulet of Water will not save us if the other two fall into the wrong hands."

The Amulet of Fire: Whispers in the Dunes

"The next amulet lies far from here," Emberthane continued. "Beyond the Bershian Sea, in the Skarnith Wastes—a desert of endless dunes and ancient secrets. The Amulet of Earth rests there, buried beneath the shifting sands."

"The Skarnith Wastes?" Soren asked, her brows furrowing. "I've heard tales of that place. Travellers speak of whispers on the wind, voices that lead them astray until they vanish without a trace."

Eryndal tilted his head, intrigued despite himself. "Are the whispers real?"

"They are," Emberthane said. "The desert is steeped in magic, the remnants of an age before even the sorcerers of the amulets. Those who walk its sands speak of the voices of the dead, their secrets carried on the wind. It is said that the Amulet of Earth amplifies this magic, its presence calling to the lost and the forgotten."

Roland frowned. "Why would anyone hide an amulet there? It seems…reckless."

"The Skarnith Wastes were once a fertile kingdom," Emberthane explained. "Centuries ago, it was a land of life and plenty. But when the Wars of Old began, the kingdom fell to ruin. The sorcerer who carried the Amulet of Fire retreated there, hoping the desert's isolation would protect it. Over time, the magic of the amulet corrupted the land, draining it of life and leaving only the desolation that exists today."

"And now the desert guards it," Soren said, her voice thoughtful. "But if the amulet has been there for so long, why hasn't anyone found it?"

"The sands shift constantly," Emberthane replied. "The amulet's power moves with them, its location ever-changing. Even those who seek it with pure intentions are driven mad by the whispers, the illusions, the relentless heat. To find the Amulet of Fire is to face not only the desert's fury but one's own mind."

Eryndal straightened, his resolve clear despite the enormity of the challenge. "Then we must prepare. Whatever trials the desert has in store, we will face them together."

The Amulet of Air: The Sunken City of Vyradon

Emberthane's light dimmed slightly as it spoke again, its tone sombre. "The final amulet lies beneath the waves. The Amulet of Air rests in the ruins of Vyradon, a city swallowed by the ocean centuries ago. Once, it was a place of beauty and innovation, the crown jewel of the eastern seas. But its ambition became its downfall."

"What happened to it?" Soren asked, her tone laced with curiosity.

"It is said that Vyradon's rulers sought to harness the power of the winds and the skies," Emberthane said. "They created devices to manipulate the air, to control the very weather itself. But their experiments angered the gods—or so the legends say. The sea rose against them, swallowing the city whole. Only ruins remain, hidden in the depths."

"And the amulet?" Roland asked.

"The Amulet of Air was taken there by another sorcerer," Emberthane replied. "She believed that hiding it beneath the waves would protect it from the chaos above. But the city's magic, combined with the amulet's power, has created something…unnatural. The waters around Vyradon are treacherous, filled with storms that rage without end. Those who venture too close speak of strange creatures lurking beneath the waves, their forms twisted by the amulet's influence."

Eryndal's brow furrowed. "Creatures? What kind of creatures?"

"Things that should not exist," Emberthane said. "Some say they are the remnants of Vyradon's people, transformed by the magic of the amulet. Others believe they are guardians, created by the sorcerer to ensure the amulet remains hidden. Whatever the truth, none who have seen them have lived to tell the tale."

Soren crossed her arms, her eyes narrowing. "And we're supposed to find this amulet in the middle of an endless storm, surrounded by creatures from a nightmare? Lovely."

"It will not be easy," Emberthane said. "But the amulet's power cannot be allowed to remain unchecked. If Raxis's followers find it, they will use it to spread their influence across the seas, cutting off trade, travel, and alliances. The world would be isolated, vulnerable to their plans."

The Path Forward

The companions fell into a tense silence, the enormity of their task weighing heavily on them. Each amulet was not only a source of immense power but a harbinger of danger, hidden in places where survival was not guaranteed.

"We must move quickly," Emberthane said, breaking the silence. "Raxis's followers are not idle. They already possess the Amulet of Water, and they will stop at nothing to claim the others."

Roland's gaze hardened; his resolve unwavering. "Then we'll stop them. No matter the cost, we'll find the amulets first."

Soren nodded, her sharp eyes glinting with determination. "And we'll make sure they never fall into the wrong hands again."

Eryndal rested his hand on his staff, his voice steady. "This journey will test us. But together, we can succeed."

Emberthane's form flickered, its light growing brighter. "Then let us not waste time. The path is long, and the stakes are high. But if we stand united, there is still hope for this world."

As they resumed their climb, the companions carried with them the knowledge of the amulets' locations—a map of peril and promise. Each step brought them closer to their destiny and their bond strengthened by the challenges ahead. They were no longer just adventurers; they were protectors, united by purpose and bound by fate.

The journey to the Skarnith Wastes, the Blackwater Marshes, and the sunken city of Vyradon awaited them, each more dangerous than the last. And though the road was uncertain, one truth remained clear: the fate of the world rested in their hands.

The Dark Magic of the Mountains

The climb grew steeper, the jagged rocks beneath their feet slick with frost and uneven from centuries of shifting earth. The air was thin, biting at their exposed skin and turning every breath into a visible puff of mist. Yet it was not the cold that set the companions on edge; it was the sensation that the mountains themselves were alive, watching, and waiting.

The deeper they ventured into the peaks, the more oppressive the atmosphere became. The crisp mountain air, once invigorating, was now thick and cloying, carrying an unnatural chill that seemed to sink into their very bones. A faint mist clung to the ground, swirling in ghostly patterns that vanished as quickly as they appeared.

Soren tightened her cloak around her shoulders, her sharp eyes scanning the terrain. "Does anyone else feel like we're being watched?"

Roland grunted, his hand never straying far from the hilt of his sword. "Watched, followed, hunted—take your pick. I don't trust these peaks."

Eryndal remained silent, his staff in hand as he focused on the path ahead. But his furrowed brow and tight grip betrayed his unease.

As they ascended further, the whispers began.

The Whispers in the Wind

At first, the sounds were faint, almost imperceptible—soft murmurs that blended with the howling of the wind. But as they climbed, the voices grew clearer, weaving in and out of hearing like a half-remembered dream.

"What is that?" Soren asked, stopping in her tracks. Her voice was steady, but her wide eyes betrayed her fear.

"Dark magic," Eryndal replied grimly, his usually calm demeanour shaken. "It's in the air, trying to divide us."

The whispers danced just beyond their understanding, slipping through the cracks of reason like water through clenched fingers. They didn't seem to come from any one direction, instead surrounding them, pressing into their minds. Shadows flitted along the edges of their vision, moving too quickly to be real.

Then the voices changed.

The Voices of the Past

For Eryndal, the whispers coalesced into the unmistakable voice of his father.

"You'll never be strong enough, boy," the voice sneered, cold and biting like the wind around him. "Your magic is weak. You're weak."

Eryndal's steps faltered, his grip on his staff tightening until his knuckles turned white. He shook his head, trying to dispel the voice, but it persisted, growing louder.

For Roland, the voices took on a different, far more devastating form.

"Father, help me!" cried the voice of his son. The anguished tone cut through him like a blade, each word a fresh wound. Roland froze in place, his breath hitching as the screams filled his ears. He could see the memory of that terrible day so vividly—the monster, his son's final moments, his own failure to save him.

And for Soren, the whispers spoke of betrayal.

"Coward," they hissed, their tones shifting between the voices of her kin. "You left us. You abandoned your people to save yourself."

Soren staggered as if struck, the weight of the accusations crushing her. Though she knew the voices were lies, her heart still ached with guilt.

The group began to splinter, each of them consumed by their own torment. The dark magic fed on their fears and regrets, digging into the deepest parts of their minds to sow division and doubt.

The Breaking Point

"Don't listen to them!" Eryndal shouted, his voice cutting through the swirling wind. "It's not real. It's trying to turn us against each other."

But his words barely reached them. Roland remained rooted in place, his fists clenched and trembling, his sword hanging uselessly at his side. His breaths were shallow and ragged as if he were drowning in the memories.

Soren had fallen to her knees, her face pale and drawn. Her hands pressed against her temples as if trying to block out the voices, but they only grew louder, more insistent.

Eryndal gritted his teeth, his own father's voice still echoing in his mind. He raised his staff, the runes etched along its length flaring to life with a faint blue light. Summoning every ounce of his will, he muttered a counterspell, his voice trembling but determined.

The light from his staff pushed back the shadows slightly, but it was not enough. The magic of the mountains was ancient and insidious, its tendrils woven into the very fabric of the peaks.

Emberthane Intervenes

It was then that Emberthane acted.

The guardian's glowing form, which had been dim and subdued in the presence of the dark magic, suddenly flared with brilliant light. Emberthane shifted into a humanoid shape, its translucent eyes blazing like twin stars. Its voice rang out, not in the language of the companions but in a tongue older than the mountains themselves. The words resonated in the air, their power palpable, vibrating through the stone beneath their feet.

The shadows recoiled, writhing like living things as Emberthane's light consumed them. The whispers faltered, their voices growing distant and indistinct before fading entirely.

As the oppressive magic lifted, the companions gasped, their minds suddenly clear. Roland stumbled forward, his hand clutching his chest as if trying to steady his heart. Soren rose shakily to her feet, her eyes darting around as if searching for lingering threats.

Eryndal lowered his staff, his shoulders slumping with exhaustion. "What…what was that?" He asked, his voice hoarse.

"This place is tainted by the shadows of the past," Emberthane said, its voice steady but tinged with sorrow. "The magic of the amulets once flowed through these mountains. Though the sorcerers are long gone, their influence remains, festering like an open wound."

The Lingering Unease

Though the immediate danger had passed, the companions could not shake the unease that lingered in the air. The mountains felt colder and darker as if the shadows themselves resented their presence.

Roland glanced at Emberthane; his voice rough. "If that's just the remnants of the magic, what happens when we get closer to the source?"

"The danger will only grow," Emberthane replied. "The amulets' power calls to all who come near, good and evil alike. The darkness you faced just now was but a whisper of what lies ahead."

Soren crossed her arms, her expression hard. "Then we'll have to be stronger. Whatever this magic throws at us, we can't afford to give in."

"She's right," Eryndal said, his voice steadier now. "This magic feeds on fear, on doubt. If we let it consume us, we'll fail."

Emberthane's light dimmed slightly, as if in thought. "You have shown resilience, but the trials ahead will test you in ways you cannot yet imagine. Trust in one another and remember that the whispers are lies meant to break you."

Pressing Forward

With Emberthane's guidance, the group pressed onward, their steps slower but more deliberate. The path grew narrower, the cliffs on either side plunging into darkness. The wind howled louder, carrying faint traces of the whispers they thought they had left behind.

Though the companions were silent, the tension among them was palpable. The dark magic had planted seeds of doubt, and though they tried to ignore them, the scars remained.

Roland walked to the front of the group, his hand resting on the hilt of his sword. His son's screams still echoed faintly in his mind, a cruel reminder of his failure. But he clenched his jaw and pressed on, determined not to let the past define him.

Soren followed closely behind, her sharp eyes scanning the shadows for signs of danger. The voices of her kin still lingered, accusing her of abandoning them. But she steeled herself, knowing that the only way to atone for her mistakes was to succeed in the journey ahead.

Eryndal brought up the rear, his staff glowing faintly to light the path. His father's voice still rang in his ears, calling him weak. But he knew better now. The whispers were lies, and he would not let them control him.

And at the centre of it all was Emberthane, its light a beacon in the darkness. Though the guardian had banished the immediate threat, it could feel the mountains watching, waiting. The battle for the amulets had only just begun, and the companions would need every ounce of strength, courage, and unity to overcome the trials ahead.

The dark magic of the mountains was a force to be reckoned with, but together, they would face it—and they would not falter.

Chapter 10
The Screams in the Dark

As the companions descended into the valley within the Varnor Mountains, an unshakeable sense of unease crept over them. The mist clung to their cloaks like a living thing, cool tendrils of vapour coiling around their arms and legs, making every step feel heavier than it should have. The sun, hidden behind a dense canopy of swirling clouds, offered no warmth or solace, and the air was cold enough to cut their breath short. Emberthane, whose glow had been a constant reassurance in their travels, now flickered faintly, as if the dark energy of the valley sought to snuff it out entirely.

"This place feels wrong," Roland muttered, his voice barely audible over the low whistle of the wind.

Eryndal gripped his staff tightly, the runes along its length glowing faintly as he muttered an incantation to ward off any nearby threats. "It's more than wrong," he replied grimly. "There's a presence here—a shadow that clings to the very air. Stay alert."

Ahead of them, the mist parted to reveal a sight that made their blood run cold: a settlement, or what was left of one. Broken homes lay scattered across the valley like the bones of some great beast, their wooden walls clawed apart and their stone foundations blackened as if burned. The ground was soaked with blood, its coppery tang thick in the air, and bodies lay where they had fallen, twisted and torn beyond recognition.

Roland's hand went instinctively to the hilt of his sword. "What happened here?" He growled, though he already knew the answer in his heart.

A Sanctuary Lost

Emberthane stepped forward, its translucent form flickering with what could only be described as grief. "This place...I know it," the guardian said, its voice tinged with sorrow. "Long ago, before I became what I am, I lived among the people who called this valley home."

The others turned to look at Emberthane, surprise etched on their faces.

"They were a hidden colony," it continued, its glowing eyes scanning the ruins with a distant, haunted gaze. "They sought refuge here, far from the chaos of the outside world. They were peaceful, isolated, and secretive. They trusted no one—not the kingdoms of men, not the elven clans, not the wandering merchants who passed through the mountains. They swore allegiance only to life itself."

"And now?" Soren asked softly, though she feared the answer.

Emberthane's light dimmed further. "Now, they are gone. Slaughtered. Their sanctuary has been defiled, turned into a place of death."

Soren bent down to examine one of the bodies, her usually sharp and confident demeanour faltering. The corpse was that of a woman, her face frozen in an expression of pure terror. Deep gashes ran across her chest, as though made by claws, and the symbol of a serpent eating its own tail was burned into her forehead.

"This mark," Soren said, pointing to the sigil, "it's the same mark that's been appearing all over Reldad. Raxis's followers were here."

"They weren't just here," Roland said, his voice tight with barely controlled rage. He gestured to the ground around them. "They left their message in blood. They want us to know this was their work."

The Ritual Site

The group moved cautiously through the village, their weapons at the ready. It didn't take long to discover the centrepiece of the horror: a stone altar standing in the centre of the settlement, slick with blood. Around it, strange symbols had been carved into the ground, their lines filled with crimson that glistened as if fresh. The bodies of the villagers had been arranged around the altar in grotesque patterns, their lifeless forms twisted to create a spiral that converged on the stone platform.

"This wasn't just a slaughter," Eryndal said, his voice trembling. "This was a ritual."

Emberthane approached the altar, its form growing brighter as it inspected the markings. "These symbols...they're ancient. Older than even I can remember. They speak of summoning, of binding life to something far darker than death."

Soren's face grew pale as she knelt beside one of the symbols. "I can feel the magic still pulsing through these lines. It's strong—stronger than anything I've ever encountered. Whoever did this wasn't just trying to kill. They were trying to call something."

Roland's grip tightened on his sword as he stepped closer to the altar, his expression dark. "And where is it now? If they summoned something, why isn't it here?"

Eryndal frowned. "Perhaps the ritual wasn't completed, or perhaps whatever they called is already gone. Either way, the fact that they attempted this at all means they're growing bolder."

Emberthane's light flared, its voice heavy with anger. "This was not just an attempt. This was a warning. Raxis's followers wanted us to see this, to know the lengths they would go to. The souls of these villagers have been sacrificed for their cause, their lives stolen to feed the dark magic that binds this land."

The Whispers Begin

As they stood in the centre of the ruined village, the wind began to pick up, carrying with it a sound that made the hairs on the back of their necks stand on end. Low and guttural at first, the sound grew louder and more distinct, until it became clear: it was the sound of voices.

They weren't human voices, though; they were warped, echoing whispers that seemed to come from everywhere and nowhere at once. The words were unintelligible, but the malice behind them was unmistakable.

"What is that?" Soren asked, her voice trembling.

"It's the screams of the dead," Emberthane said grimly. "The souls of the villagers are still here, bound by the ritual. They cannot rest."

As if in response to Emberthane's words, the whispers grew louder, morphing into a cacophony of anguished cries. The mist around them thickened, coiling like smoke, and shapes began to form within it—shadowy figures that writhed and twisted, their features obscured but their torment evident.

Eryndal raised his staff, muttering a protective spell as the figures moved closer. "These are no ordinary spirits. They've been corrupted by the dark magic of this place. We need to be careful."

The Screams in the Dark

The shadowy figures circled the group, their cries growing louder until they became deafening. Each member of the group began to hear something different within the cacophony—voices that were achingly familiar, speaking words designed to pierce their hearts.

For Roland, it was the voice of his son, screaming his name in terror. The sound sent him reeling, his grip on his sword faltering. "No," he muttered, his voice choked with emotion. "This isn't real. It can't be."

For Soren, it was the voices of her kin, accusing her of abandoning them, of turning her back on her people. The weight of their words made her stagger, her dagger slipping from her grasp. "I didn't—" she began, but the voices drowned her out.

Eryndal heard the voice of his father, a stern and disapproving tone that had haunted him since his youth.

"You've failed, Eryndal. You were never strong enough. You've doomed them all."

The whispers clawed at their minds, feeding on their fears and insecurities, dragging them deeper into despair.

Emberthane's Light

Amid the chaos, Emberthane flared brightly, its form expanding until it was a blazing beacon of light. "Enough!" it cried, its voice resonating like a thunderclap.

The shadows recoiled, their forms unravelling like smoke in the wind. The whispers faded, leaving only the sound of the wind and the companions' ragged breaths.

Emberthane's light dimmed slightly as it turned to the group. "This is the power of Raxis's followers," it said. "They twist the souls of the innocent to serve their dark purpose. But we cannot let them win. We must stay strong, or we will become their next victims."

Roland nodded, his grip tightening on his sword. "We won't let them break us."

Though the shadows had been banished, the weight of the village's tragedy lingered.

The Screams

Eryndal stood motionless amid the devastation of the ruined village, the jagged wind pulling at his robes as the others scoured the wreckage for supplies or clues. To them, the valley was eerily silent save for the occasional creak of broken wood or the faint howling of the wind through the gashes in the ruins. But for Eryndal, it was anything but silent.

He tilted his head slightly, his brow furrowing as a deep, unsettling sound reached his ears. It wasn't the mournful cry of the wind or the distant rumble of falling rocks. It was something far more personal, more visceral.

Screams

They clawed at the edges of his mind, high-pitched and agonised, yet interspersed with something hauntingly familiar. These weren't screams designed to terrify or repel intruders; they were cries of raw suffering, of pain so profound that it seemed to stretch across time and space. They didn't just echo in his ears; they resonated in his chest, pulling at some deep, untouched part of his soul.

He couldn't explain it, but the screams weren't entirely alien to him. There was a sense of recognition, a faint connection that he couldn't place but also couldn't ignore. Before he realised it, his feet had begun to move, following the source of the cries.

Eryndal's grip tightened on his staff, the familiar weight of the ancient wood grounding him as his steps grew softer, almost hesitant. He didn't want to disturb whatever lay ahead, nor did he want to alert the others. He told himself they wouldn't understand, that they were too focused on the immediate dangers of their quest to feel the pull of these tortured sounds.

But the truth was simpler: he didn't want them to stop him.

The Monster

The screams led him to the edge of the village, where the ruins ended abruptly at a series of jagged cliffs that fell away into mist-shrouded depths.

The wind here was colder, sharper, carrying with it a faint metallic tang that made the back of his throat burn.

Nestled in the shadow of a large boulder, he saw it.

At first, he thought it was another victim, perhaps a survivor who had managed to crawl away from the carnage. It was small, barely the size of a child, and its body was hunched over as it shook with heaving sobs. But as Eryndal stepped closer, the figure came into sharper focus, and his breath caught in his throat.

It *was* a child—or at least, it had been. The boy couldn't have been more than ten years old, but his body was grotesquely distorted. His arms bulged with muscles that seemed too large for his frame, his skin stretched thin over the unnatural growths. Scars crisscrossed his face, long and jagged as if carved by claws. One of his eyes was swollen and oversized, glowing faintly like a cyclopean orb, its reddish hue casting an eerie light over the surrounding rock.

Eryndal's heart ached at the sight. Despite the monstrous features, the boy's humanity was still visible in the way he wept, his shoulders shaking with each sob. This wasn't a monster—it was a child. A broken, hurting, and lonely child.

"Hey," Eryndal said softly, his voice gentle as he stepped forward. "It's okay. I'm not here to hurt you."

The boy didn't respond, his sobs continuing unabated. Eryndal's instincts as a healer kicked in, and he lowered his staff, holding out a hand as if approaching a wounded animal. "I can help you. You're not alone anymore."

At the sound of his voice, the boy suddenly went still. The sobs stopped, replaced by an unnatural silence that made the hairs on Eryndal's neck stand on end. Slowly, the child turned his head to look at him, and Eryndal's heart sank further.

The boy's glowing eye burned brighter, the red light intensifying as his face contorted into a snarl. A guttural scream erupted from his throat, echoing across the cliffs with a sound that was neither human nor beast.

Then, his body began to change.

The Transformation

Eryndal stumbled back as the boy's frame contorted, his small body elongating and twisting in ways that defied nature. The oversized muscles swelled further, tearing through his tattered clothes, and the scars on his skin split open to reveal jagged bone protrusions that jutted out like crude armour.

The single glowing eye expanded, its light growing more intense until it became a blazing orb of crimson fire. The boy's hands grew into claws, their edges sharp enough to gleam even in the dim light, and his feet lengthened into hooves that struck the ground with a deafening crack.

Within seconds, the boy was gone. In his place stood a towering monstrosity, its hulking form radiating raw, uncontrollable power. The ground trembled beneath its massive frame, and its roar shattered the eerie stillness of the valley, sending flocks of birds screeching into the air.

Eryndal's breath came in shallow gasps as he scrambled backwards, his staff raised defensively. "Wait!" he called out, his voice trembling. "I'm not your enemy! Please, listen to me!"

But the creature was beyond reason. The agony and despair that had once driven its cries had now transformed into unbridled rage, and it charged at Eryndal with terrifying speed.

The Fight

Eryndal barely managed to roll out of the way as the giant's massive fist slammed into the ground where he had been standing. The impact sent a shockwave through the earth, knocking him off his feet and sending loose rocks tumbling down the cliffs.

Back in the village, the others heard the commotion and turned towards the sound.

"Eryndal!" Roland shouted, his eyes narrowing as he spotted the giant looming over their companion in the distance. Without hesitation, he drew his sword and sprinted towards the cliffs, Soren close on his heels.

When they arrived, they found Eryndal pinned against a boulder, the giant advancing on him with murderous intent. Its burning eye focused on him with unrelenting fury, and its claws scraped against the stone as it prepared to strike.

Roland didn't hesitate. With a battle cry, he charged forward, his blade slicing through the air as he aimed for the giant's exposed back. The sword struck true, biting into the creature's flesh and eliciting a roar of pain.

The giant whirled around, its massive arm swinging towards Roland with enough force to shatter bone. Roland managed to duck under the blow, but the force of the swing sent him sprawling to the ground.

"We have to take it down!" Roland shouted; his voice filled with urgency.

"No!" Eryndal's voice rang out, sharp and commanding. He pushed himself to his feet, his staff glowing faintly as he placed himself between the giant and the others. "It's not a monster. It's a boy. He's just...lost."

Soren hesitated; her dagger drawn but her hand trembling. "Eryndal, it's going to kill you! You can't reason with that thing!"

Eryndal didn't reply. Instead, he closed his eyes and focused on the magic within him, reaching out towards the giant with his mind.

A Glimpse of the Truth

As Eryndal's magic touched the creature, he felt a rush of emotions that nearly overwhelmed him. Pain. Sorrow. Fear. The giant's rage wasn't mindless—it was born of a deep and all-consuming despair. In its transformed state, the boy's humanity had been buried beneath layers of torment, but it was still there, faint and flickering like a dying ember.

"Listen to me," Eryndal said softly, his voice steady despite the chaos around him. "I know you're hurting. I know you're scared. But you don't have to fight. You don't have to be alone."

The giant hesitated, its massive chest heaving as it stared down at Eryndal with its blazing eye. For a moment, the rage seemed to waver, and the creature let out a low, guttural sound that was almost a whimper.

But the moment didn't last. With a roar, the giant turned and fled, its massive strides shaking the ground as it disappeared into the mist-shrouded mountains.

Aftermath

The companions stood in stunned silence; their weapons still drawn as the echoes of the giant's retreat faded into the distance.

Roland was the first to speak. "What was that?" He asked, his voice filled with a mix of confusion and anger.

"It was a boy," Eryndal said quietly, his gaze fixed on the spot where the creature had vanished. "Twisted by magic and pain, but still a boy."

Soren sheathed her dagger, her expression troubled. "If that's what Raxis's magic does to children, what else is it capable of?"

Emberthane, who had arrived just in time to see the creature's retreat, spoke gravely. "This is only the beginning. The darkness that taints this land is growing stronger, and it will consume everything if we don't stop it."

Eryndal nodded, his grip on his staff tightening. "Then we can't afford to falter. We have to find a way to stop it before more lives are lost."

As the companions gathered together, the wind carried the faintest echo of the boy's screams—still lingering in the air like a warning.

A Mystery Unfolds

As the dust from the creature's retreat settled, the companions slowly gathered around Eryndal, their faces a mix of concern, disbelief, and lingering shock. The echoes of the creature's footsteps faded into the distant mountains, but the air felt thick with the aftermath of their encounter. The wind had died down, leaving behind an eerie stillness that seemed to stretch on for miles, as if the valley itself was holding its breath.

Soren, ever the practical one, was the first to speak. Her voice trembled, and despite her usual composure, there was a note of fear beneath her words. "What just happened? That thing. That *monster*—it was a child. A child twisted into something unrecognisable. How could that even happen?"

Her wide eyes darted between Eryndal and the ruins, seeking some answer, any explanation, but none came easily. The unsettling reality of what they had witnessed weighed heavily on them all. The creature's gargantuan form, its glowing, bloodshot eye, the sheer violence of its movements—none of it made sense. Yet, despite the destruction it had wrought, Eryndal's insistence that the boy was still in there, somewhere, lingered in the air like a shadow.

Eryndal leaned heavily on his staff, his face pale and drawn. His usual calm demeanour had been shattered by the harrowing encounter. He could still feel the boy's pain, the sheer sorrow that had pulsed through him like a living thing, and it tugged at his heart in ways he couldn't fully explain. He closed his eyes for a moment, trying to collect his thoughts, but the memory of the boy's eyes—so full of suffering and rage—remained vivid in his mind.

"That boy," he began, his voice quiet but filled with determination. "He's part of this. I don't know how, but he is. And we need to find him again." His voice faltered slightly, and he glanced at the ground as if searching for some piece of the puzzle that could bring him clarity.

Roland, his brow furrowed in frustration, shook his head. He couldn't bring himself to understand. "Whatever he is, he's dangerous. We barely survived that. That thing—*whatever* it was—almost killed us, Eryndal. It doesn't matter that he was once a child; he nearly ripped us apart." His grip on his sword tightened, his knuckles white, the anger and confusion swirling inside him like a storm. "We can't just go after him again. You saw what happened."

Eryndal's gaze remained steady, his eyes meeting Roland's with a quiet resolve. "But he's not evil," Eryndal insisted, his voice growing firmer as he spoke. "That boy isn't a monster. He's just lost." His hands clenched tightly around his staff as though trying to hold onto something intangible, something that could make sense of the chaos that had unfolded. "He's trapped in something far worse than we can imagine. But he's trying to tell us something. He was reaching out for help, even in his twisted form. And if we don't find him, if we don't try to help, he will remain like that forever, a prisoner of whatever dark magic corrupted him."

Soren, though more inclined to take a pragmatic approach, couldn't entirely ignore the depth of Eryndal's conviction. The fear in his voice, the haunted look in his eyes—it wasn't like him to act so desperate. And something about the encounter felt different, too. There had been something human in the creature, something she couldn't ignore. She glanced back at the cliffside where the boy-turned-monster had fled, her dagger still in her hand, though its tip now hovered just above the ground.

"But how do you know he's not beyond saving?" She asked quietly, her voice barely above a whisper. "How can you be sure that he hasn't already become whatever twisted thing that magic intended him to be? We don't know what we're dealing with here. We could be chasing ghosts, Eryndal."

Eryndal turned to face Soren, his expression sombre but unwavering. "Because the magic that transformed him, that twisted him into something monstrous, is not entirely of this world. I felt it—the way it clawed at him, reshaped him, warped his mind. It's ancient and dark, but it *can* be undone. I believe it can be undone. But we have to find him, we have to reach him before it consumes him entirely."

Roland, still sceptical but unwilling to dismiss Eryndal's wisdom entirely, crossed his arms over his chest. He looked back towards the distant horizon, where the fading sun cast long shadows over the mountains. "And if we find him, what then? What's the next step? How do we even begin to undo what's been done to him?" His voice carried a mix of frustration and uncertainty, but there was also something else there—an unspoken hope. Roland didn't want to believe that the boy was beyond saving, but the events of the last few minutes weighed heavily on him.

Emberthane, who had remained eerily silent throughout the encounter, finally spoke. Its glowing form flickered, brighter for a moment as it added its own voice to the conversation. "The dark magic in this place has twisted many souls," it said slowly, its voice as grave as the mountains themselves. "But you are right, Eryndal. That boy is not beyond saving. And perhaps, in saving him, we may find the answers we seek."

The words hung in the air, heavy with meaning. The group exchanged uneasy glances, each of them silently considering the possibility that what they had seen was just the beginning of something far more insidious. The boy—*the creature*—was just one piece of the puzzle. But how far did the puzzle stretch? What other horrors lay hidden in the depths of the valley, waiting to be uncovered?

Eryndal's thoughts began to race again. *The boy, despite his transformation, had still been aware—he had understood that someone had reached out to him. There was still hope, however faint. But what of the dark magic? What was its true purpose? Was this boy a victim, or was he part of something far larger than they could imagine?* The questions swirled in his mind, impossible to answer at that moment, but all the more pressing because of it.

As the companions regrouped, their minds heavy with uncertainty, they prepared to move on. The sound of the boy's screams—the raw, guttural cries of pain and fear—still echoed in Eryndal's thoughts, drowning out the other sounds of the valley. He could feel it. He could feel that the boy was still out there, still somewhere in this forsaken place, calling for help.

The journey ahead had just grown more complicated—and more dangerous.

"We need to keep moving," Emberthane urged, its voice cutting through the silence that had settled over the group. "The boy may still be near. But more importantly, there are other dangers here—dangers that we are not prepared for. If we linger too long, we may find ourselves trapped in this place with no way out."

Roland nodded reluctantly, the weight of the decision settling in his chest. "Then we move. But we keep our eyes open. We're not leaving without answers."

As they moved deeper into the valley, each step seemed to bring them closer to something unknown, something far darker than they had anticipated. They could not afford to fail. They couldn't afford to allow the boy's suffering to be in vain. And they couldn't ignore the reality that, whatever forces were at work in these cursed lands, they were powerful, relentless, and far beyond the understanding of any of them.

The mystery was unfolding before them, one painful step at a time. And with every passing moment, the shadows of the past seemed to grow longer, darker, and more determined to consume everything in their path.

Chapter 11
The Cursed Son

The ground trembled with the echoes of the giant's retreating footsteps, but the air remained heavy as if the land itself mourned the creature's presence. The companions stood amidst the ruins, their breaths visible in the cold air, every sound amplified by the oppressive silence. Eryndal's knuckles were white around his staff, his pulse still racing from the encounter. Though the monstrous form was gone, his mind lingered on the boy within it—the fragile humanity buried beneath layers of grotesque transformation.

"We have to go on as Emberthane said but we need to go back, we can't leave him out there," Eryndal said firmly, breaking the tense quiet. His voice held an uncharacteristic edge, his usual calm replaced by something more urgent.

Roland wheeled on him, his sword still in hand, as though expecting the creature to return at any moment. "Are you mad?" He demanded, his voice rising with disbelief. "That *thing*—that *boy*—just tried to kill you. To kill *all* of us. You want to go after it? No, Eryndal, we're lucky we got out of that alive."

"It wasn't trying to kill us," Soren interjected, stepping closer to Eryndal. Her voice was steadier, but her gaze betrayed the same unease that had settled over all of them. "Not really. It was scared—confused. You saw its eyes, Roland. That wasn't rage; that was pain."

Roland scoffed, gesturing towards the distant cliffs where the creature had disappeared. "Pain? Is that what you call crushing the earth with fists the size of a wagon? I don't care what it *used to be*—whatever magic did this to him has made him dangerous. We can't trust him."

Soren squared her shoulders, her emerald eyes glinting with defiance. "And what would you suggest we do? Walk away? Leave him to rot in whatever darkness turned him into that?"

"Yes," Roland replied sharply, his frustration boiling over. "If it means keeping us alive, yes."

Eryndal's voice rose above the brewing argument, his tone commanding enough to draw both of their attention. "Enough! This isn't about trust, and it isn't about fear. That boy is as much a victim as anyone else in this cursed place." He fixed Roland with a steely gaze, his words carrying a weight that even the battle-hardened swordsman couldn't dismiss. "You saw the symbols in the village. You saw the magic they used. Whatever did this to him—it's connected to Raxis. He's part of this puzzle, whether we like it or not."

Roland opened his mouth to argue but closed it again, his jaw tightening as he looked away.

Emberthane, who had remained silent during the exchange, drifted closer, its light dimming slightly as it spoke. "Eryndal is right. The boy's transformation is not a natural one, nor is it permanent. This is a curse wrought by ancient magic; a magic tied to Raxis's rising power. If we abandon him now, we lose not only a chance to save him but perhaps a key to understanding the greater threat we face."

The silence that followed was thick with tension, but no one voiced further dissent. Roland sheathed his sword with a heavy sigh, though his eyes remained wary. Soren nodded at Eryndal, her expression softening.

"Then we follow," she said simply.

The Hidden Power

The companions followed the trail left by the giant; its massive footprints pressed deep into the frozen earth. The path wound through jagged cliffs and narrow passes, the terrain growing more treacherous with each step. The air grew colder, biting at their skin and numbing their fingers, and the shadows seemed to stretch longer as if watching their every move. Whispers flitted on the wind, low and unintelligible, like echoes of forgotten words.

"This place is alive with magic," Emberthane observed, its glow casting long shadows on the rocky walls around them. "Not just dark magic—older, wilder magic. It clings to these mountains like frost to stone."

As they rounded a bend, the trail led them to a wide, desolate plateau where the ground was littered with jagged stones and skeletal trees. In the distance, silhouetted against the faint light of the moon, was the giant. It was crouched at the edge of a deep chasm, its massive shoulders heaving as though caught in the throes of despair.

"There," Eryndal whispered, his heart pounding.

Soren's hand drifted to her dagger; her movements cautious as she scanned the area. Roland stood tense, one hand on his sword hilt, his eyes locked on the creature.

Eryndal took a steadying breath and stepped forward. "Let me try something," he said, his voice low but firm.

"What?" Roland hissed; his tone edged with disbelief. "You can't be serious. You're going to—what—*talk* to it?"

Eryndal ignored him. He gripped his staff tightly, its faint glow growing stronger as he approached the creature. His heart raced with every step, but his resolve remained firm. He didn't know what he was about to do, but he knew he had to try.

When he was close enough, he stopped and focused on the giant. He could feel the dark magic swirling around it, a storm of anguish and chaos that lashed out in all directions. Closing his eyes, he reached out with his own magic, extending a thread of light into the maelstrom.

The connection hit him like a physical blow. His mind was flooded with images—fragmented, jarring memories that weren't his own. He saw flashes of a life before the curse: a young man not much older than himself, leading an army into battle. Then came the darkness—shadows descending, a circle of robed figures chanting in a language older than time, the boy's screams as the transformation began.

Eryndal gasped, staggering under the weight of the memories. But he didn't let go. He focused on the boy—the flicker of light buried deep within the darkness. It was faint, almost extinguished, but it was still there.

"Stay with me," he murmured, his voice barely audible. "I know you're in there. Let me help you."

The giant roared, its massive hands clutching its head as it thrashed in agony. The ground shook beneath its weight, and the companions tensed, ready to intervene.

"Eryndal, get back!" Roland shouted, but Soren held him back.

"He's helping him," she said, her voice hushed but steady.

Eryndal pressed harder, pouring his own magic into the connection. He felt the darkness begin to loosen its grip, the bonds of the curse fraying under the strain. The flicker of light grew stronger, pushing back against the shadows.

With a final, guttural cry, the giant collapsed, its massive form shrinking and twisting as the magic unravelled. The companions watched in stunned silence as the hulking creature was replaced by a small, trembling figure—a boy no older than ten, his body thin and frail, his skin marred by scars.

The Cursed Son

The boy lay curled on the ground, his chest heaving as though he'd just run a great distance. His single, glowing eye was gone, replaced by two tear-filled eyes that darted around in confusion.

Eryndal knelt beside him, his heart aching at the sight. "It's okay," he said softly, his voice as gentle as he could make it. "You're safe now."

The boy flinched at the sound, his thin arms wrapping around his knees as though trying to make himself smaller.

Roland stood a few paces back, his arms crossed as he watched the scene unfold. "What now?" He asked, his tone neutral but laced with unease.

Emberthane floated closer, its light illuminating the boy's scarred face. "This child is a victim, but he is also a vessel," it said gravely. "The magic that cursed him was meant to twist him into a weapon—a weapon of Raxis. But he resisted, even in his monstrous form. That resistance may be the key to breaking the cycle of darkness that holds this land."

The boy looked up at Emberthane, his tear-streaked face a mixture of fear and awe. "I didn't want to hurt anyone," he said, his voice breaking. "I tried to stop it, but I couldn't..."

"You didn't fail," Eryndal said firmly, meeting the boy's gaze. "You're here now. That's what matters."

The boy's eyes filled with fresh tears, and he buried his face in his hands.

The Boy Returns

Soren was the first to move, rushing to the boy's side with a swiftness born of instinct. The chill in the air seemed sharper now, pressing against them like a blade as the boy shivered violently. Without hesitation, she unfastened her cloak and wrapped it around his trembling frame. The fabric, though rough, was warm and smelled faintly of earth and leather—a small comfort against the unforgiving cold.

He looked up at her, his wide eyes glistening with tears. The faint glow of Emberthane's light revealed the streaks of dirt and scars that marred his face, evidence of a life steeped in hardship. His voice was a raspy whisper, barely audible above the sigh of the wind.

"Thank you," he said, his words trembling as much as his small body.

Eryndal who was kneeling beside him; his staff planted firmly in the ground for support. His expression was soft yet searching, his blue eyes scanning the boy's face for something beyond the physical. "What's your name?" He asked, his tone calm but deliberate.

The boy hesitated, his lips parting as though the answer were caught somewhere deep in his mind, a relic of a life he had almost forgotten. Finally, he spoke, "Aravon."

"Aravon," Soren repeated gently, her voice steady and soothing. "You're safe now."

But the boy shook his head, his small hands clutching the edges of the cloak tightly as if to anchor himself. "No one is safe," he whispered, his voice thick with grief and fear. "Not as long as my mother and father live."

The words hung in the air, heavy and cold. The group exchanged startled glances, the unspoken question passing silently between them.

"Your mother and father?" Soren asked carefully, her voice gentle but laced with unease.

Aravon lowered his gaze, his thin fingers digging into the fabric of the cloak. His voice was barely above a whisper, yet it carried the weight of countless years of pain. "Morva Sable and Raxis. I'm their son."

The silence that followed was deafening.

A Cursed Existence

It took several minutes before Aravon spoke again. The boy seemed to gather himself, the tremble in his hands easing as he recounted his story, though his voice remained unsteady.

"Long ago," he began, staring at the ground as if afraid to meet their eyes, "I served my father. I was his loyal son. I marched with his armies. I burned villages and destroyed lives—all for his glory. At first, I didn't understand what I was doing. I thought I was doing what sons were supposed to do. But then."

He paused, his brow furrowing as his voice grew quieter. "When I saw the suffering—the people screaming, begging for mercy—I started to doubt him. I started to doubt myself."

His small fists clenched; his knuckles white. "He noticed. He always noticed. My doubts made me weak in his eyes, and my weakness made me dangerous. That's when my mother stepped in."

"Morva Sable," Eryndal murmured, his face grave.

Aravon nodded. "She cursed me. She said my doubts were a stain on our family, and she would make sure I never faltered again." He lifted a hand, tracing a faint scar that ran across his jaw. "The curse bound me to a monstrous form. A weapon. I became what you saw earlier—something powerful, something uncontrollable. I was their tool, used to destroy anyone who opposed them."

"And when you resisted even that?" Soren asked softly, her hand still resting on his shoulder.

"They abandoned me," Aravon said, his voice barely above a whisper. "They turned me back into…this. A boy. Trapped in this body, unable to age, unable to die. A punishment for my betrayal." He looked up, his tear-filled eyes searching theirs for understanding. "For centuries, I've wandered alone, trying to escape them. But they always find me. Their followers killed everyone who took me in."

The raw emotion in his voice struck Eryndal like a blow. The boy wasn't just cursed—he was haunted.

Roland, who had been standing apart from the group, took a step forward, his expression hard. "So you were with them once," he said, his voice low and sharp. "You fought for them. You killed for them. And now you want us to believe you've changed?"

Aravon flinched, his small frame curling inward as if to shield himself.

Soren rose to her feet, stepping between Roland and the boy. Her emerald eyes flashed with anger as she spoke. "He's a *child*, Roland. He didn't choose this. None of this is his fault."

Roland's jaw tightened, his hands balling into fists. "Child or not, he's their blood. He carries their magic. That makes him dangerous."

"I trust him," Soren said firmly, her voice cutting through the tension like a blade.

The two stared each other down, the rift between them widening with every passing moment.

A Rift Among Allies

As they resumed their journey, the weight of the argument hung heavy over the group. Soren stayed close to Aravon, her protective instincts keeping her at his side as they navigated the treacherous mountain paths. She spoke to him gently, her voice a quiet balm against the chaos that surrounded them. She offered him reassurance when he faltered, steadying him with a calm hand or a kind word.

Roland, however, kept his distance. His mistrust was evident in the way his hand never strayed far from his sword, his sharp glances a constant reminder of his unease.

Eryndal tried to mediate, walking between the two as they pressed forward. "Roland, you're not wrong to be cautious," he said quietly, his tone measured. "But Soren's right too. Aravon didn't ask for this. If we're going to stop Raxis, we need to understand what we're up against. And that means trusting him, at least a little."

Roland grunted; his gaze fixed on the path ahead. "Trust is earned, not given," he muttered.

Aravon, who had been walking a few paces behind, overheard the exchange. His shoulders slumped, the weight of Roland's words pressing down on him like a physical burden.

Soren noticed and placed a comforting hand on his back. "Ignore him," she said softly. "He'll come around."

But Aravon shook his head. "He's right," he said, his voice small. "I don't deserve your trust."

"Yes, you do," Soren insisted, her voice firm. "You've suffered enough. It's time someone believed in you."

Despite her words, the tension among the group remained palpable. Every glance, every word exchanged seemed to carry an undercurrent of doubt and fear.

The Stirring Darkness

As they ventured deeper into the mountains, the air grew colder, and the shadows seemed to stretch longer. The whispers on the wind grew louder, more insistent, like voices speaking just beyond the edge of comprehension. The mountains themselves seemed alive, the rocks and cliffs looming over them as if watching their every move.

Emberthane flickered faintly, its light dimming as it floated ahead. "We're nearing something ancient," it said, its voice tinged with unease. "A power older than even Raxis. Be on your guard."

Aravon hesitated, his small hand clutching the edge of Soren's cloak. "I've felt this before," he said, his voice trembling. "It's…them. Their magic."

Soren exchanged a worried glance with Eryndal, who tightened his grip on his staff.

"This place is more than just a battleground," Eryndal said, his voice heavy with realisation. "It's a crucible. Whatever lies ahead, it's going to test us in ways we can't imagine."

In the depths of the mountains, something ancient stirred, its presence palpable even from a distance. It was neither friend nor foe, but a force that cared nothing for the lives it touched. For Aravon and the companions, it was a reminder that their journey was far from over—and that the darkest trials still lay ahead.

The Judge of Ages

The mountain pass narrowed as the group pressed on, their breaths forming clouds in the cold, thin air. The oppressive whispers grew louder, now distinct murmurs that seemed to probe their thoughts and emotions. The sheer cliffs on either side felt like the walls of a tomb, closing in as the companions ventured deeper into the heart of the peaks.

And then, as if crossing an invisible threshold, they found themselves standing before something ancient and terrible.

The path opened into a vast, hollow chamber carved into the mountain itself. Its walls shimmered with veins of silver and gold, casting an eerie, otherworldly light. At the centre stood a colossal stone figure, its features weathered and cracked, yet its presence emanated an undeniable power. The figure was seated on a throne that seemed to grow out of the mountain, its hands resting on its knees. Despite its stillness, it felt alive.

Emberthane flickered anxiously, its glow dimming as it drifted closer. "This is him," Eryndal whispered. "The Judge. Kinzo spoke of him, but I never thought we'd meet him."

The Judge's head tilted slightly, its massive eyes glowing faintly with an amber light. Its voice rumbled through the chamber like an avalanche, low and resonant, shaking the very ground beneath them.

"Who dares enter the chamber of judgment?"

Roland instinctively stepped forward, his hand on the hilt of his sword. "We mean no disrespect. We're travellers—"

"Travellers?" The Judge interrupted, its voice laced with ancient amusement. "No. You are far more than travellers. You carry burdens, secrets, and ambitions that weigh upon you like chains. And one among you carries the mark of a curse long tied to this land."

Its glowing eyes fixed on Aravon, who cowered behind Soren. The Judge's gaze seemed to pierce through flesh and soul, stripping away pretence and revealing the truth beneath.

"Step forward, cursed one," the Judge commanded.

Soren tightened her grip on Aravon's shoulder, but he nodded, trembling as he stepped into the Judge's light.

"I know your pain," the Judge said, its voice softer now. "You were shaped by the darkness of those who gave you life. Yet you have fought to break free, to reclaim the light they tried to extinguish."

Aravon swallowed hard, his voice small but steady. "I don't know if I've broken free. I don't know if I ever can."

The Judge was silent for a long moment, its gaze shifting to the others.

The Heroes Judged

"You," the Judge said, addressing Soren. "You have chosen to protect this boy, though it brings you great risk. Why?"

Soren stepped forward; her emerald eyes unwavering as she met the Judge's gaze. "Because he's not his parents. He didn't choose this life, this curse. He deserves a chance to be more than what they made him."

The Judge nodded slowly. "And you," it said, turning to Eryndal. "You sense the power within him, the darkness and the light. Why do you trust him?"

Eryndal hesitated, his staff glowing faintly in his hand. "Because I've felt his pain," he said. "I've seen his fear and his longing for freedom. He's not a weapon—he's a child who needs a chance to find himself."

The Judge's gaze moved to Roland, who stood stiffly, his jaw tight.

"And you," the Judge said, its voice growing colder. "You doubt him. You fear him. Why?"

Roland bristled under the scrutiny but held his ground. "Because trust is dangerous. I've seen what misplaced trust can do—it gets people killed. He's their blood. That can't be ignored."

The Judge leaned forward, its massive form casting a shadow over Roland. "And yet, here you stand, unwilling to leave him behind. What does that say of your doubt?"

Roland didn't answer, his gaze dropping to the ground.

The Judge's voice grew louder, filling the chamber. "Your choices reveal much about who you are. Compassion, wisdom, doubt—each of you carries these in measure, and each plays a role in shaping your path. You have aided this boy, protected him, and shown him the hope that was denied to him for so long. For this, you are judged worthy."

The Judge's Aid

The Judge extended a massive hand, its fingers curling upward as if offering something unseen. From the air itself, a shimmering map materialised, its surface etched with glowing runes and ancient symbols.

"This map will guide you to the *Citadel of Kings and Queens, Elderion Citadel,*" the Judge said. "The seat of power for Raxis and Morva Sable. It is there you will find the heart of their strength—and their weakness."

Soren stepped forward; her hand outstretched to take the map. As her fingers brushed its surface, a surge of warmth spread through her, filling her with a renewed sense of purpose.

"But beware," the Judge continued. "The path to the citadel is fraught with trials. The darkness that lies ahead will test your resolve, your unity, and your trust in one another. Fail, and you will not survive."

Aravon, still trembling, looked up at the Judge. "Will we have your help?"

The Judge regarded him for a long moment, its glowing eyes flickering. "You have my guidance. My aid comes not in battle but in wisdom. Remember this: the power of Raxis and Morva Sable is not their own. It is borrowed from something far older, far darker. To defeat them, you must sever their connection to it."

Eryndal's brow furrowed. "What is this power they draw from?"

The Judge's voice grew low, almost reverent. "It is a force that predates even me. A power born of chaos, of the void that existed before creation. It whispers to those who seek dominion, promising them everything they desire. But its price is steep, and its loyalty is to no one."

The companions exchanged uneasy glances, the weight of the Judge's words settling over them like a shroud.

A Path Forward

The map pulsed faintly in Soren's hands, its symbols shifting as if alive. It pointed the way forward, its glowing lines tracing a path through the treacherous mountains and beyond.

"Go now," the Judge said, its voice resonating with finality. "Your journey is far from over, and the fate of this world hangs on your success. Trust in each other, even when the darkness seeks to divide you. Only together can you overcome what lies ahead."

As the group turned to leave, the Judge's presence seemed to fade, its form merging with the mountain once more. But its words lingered, echoing in their minds as they descended the path it had revealed.

Eryndal glanced at Aravon, who walked beside Soren, his small frame still wrapped in her cloak. For the first time, there was a glimmer of hope in the boy's eyes—a fragile light that might yet grow stronger.

The Citadel of Kings and Queens awaited, its dark spires rising somewhere beyond the horizon. But for the first time, the companions felt a sense of direction, a purpose that bound them together.

The road would be long, the trials many. But they had the guidance of the Judge, the trust they were building, and the fragile hope of a cursed boy who might one day reclaim his freedom.

Chapter 12
The Perilous Journey to the Citadel

The journey from the Judge's domain deep in the Varnor Mountains to the Elderion Citadel was unlike any the heroes had faced before. Guided by the cryptic map given by the Judge—a parchment imbued with enchantments that shifted and revealed paths as they travelled. They pressed forward through the perilous terrain. The map glowed faintly in Emberthane's hands, as though reacting to her magic. Yet she often entrusted its guidance to Eryndal, especially when she would disappear into the amulet. "Keep it safe," she instructed Eryndal during one such moment. "Its connection to you has already been forged. You'll know when I'm needed." her voice was distant, her figure fading into the gemstone as though she were retreating to another plane entirely. Eryndal placed the amulet around his neck, feeling the faint hum of her essence.

The First Trial: The Caves of Echoing Stone

The first challenge came as they descended into the Caves of Echoing Stone, a labyrinth of jagged tunnels carved into the heart of the mountains. The walls shimmered faintly with veins of ancient magic, and their footsteps echoed unnaturally, creating disorientating illusions of movement. It wasn't long before they encountered the Stone Sentinels, towering golen-like creatures born from the mountain itself. Their bodies were composed of jagged rocks and molten cores, their eyes glowing with the fire of ancient magic. "We cannot outrun them," Emberthane's voice whispered through the amulet around Eryndal's neck. "They are bound to this place. You must face them."

The battle was fierce. Roland charged headlong into the fray, his sword sparking against the stone creatures, but for every blow struck, the sentinels reformed themselves, stronger and more relentless. Soren darted around the lumbering forms, trying to find weaknesses in their armour.

It was Aravon who turned the tide. As one of the sentinels cornered Roland, its molten arms raised for a killing blow, Aravon let out a roar and transformed into his demonic form. His claws tore through the sentinel's core, scattering its rocky form into rubble. For a moment, the others thought the danger had passed—until Aravon turned to them, his eyes blazing with uncontrollable fury, "Aravon, fight it!" Eryndal shouted, stepping forward, his hand brushing the amulet. The soothing energy of Emberthane's magic flowed through him. Aravon froze, his demonic form trembling as though caught between rage and reason. Slowly, painfully, he reverted to his human form as the cave fell silent; Roland placed a hand on Aravon's shoulder. "You saved my life," he admitted begrudgingly. "But don't think I'll forget what you almost did."

The Second Trial: The Frostbound Plateau

Beyond the caves lay the Frostbound Plateau, a frozen wasteland where the wind howled like a living creature, carrying with it shards of ice that cut like daggers. Visibility was almost non-existent, and Emberthane's absence during this leg was keenly felt. As they trudged forward, they came upon a pack of Frost Fangs, wolf-like beasts with fur made of ice and glowing blue eyes. Their howls were bone-chilling, a magical sound that sapped the strength and willpower of anyone who heard it for too long.

The pack circled them, their icy breath visible in the frigid air. Soren used her charm to calm the lead Frost Fang, her voice soft and melodic as she reached out to its primal instincts. But even her abilities had their limits, and when one of the wolves lunged at her, it was Aravon who reacted first, transforming once more into his demonic form. This time, Aravon maintained control. He moved with calculated precision, his monstrous strength subduing the Frost Fangs without unnecessary violence. When the battle ended, he stood before the group, his form shifting seamlessly back to human.

"You're learning," Eryndal said, offering a rare smile. Even Roland gave him a grudging nod. "We might make a warrior out of you yet."

The Third Trial: The Bridge of Shadows

The final trial was the most harrowing. The map led them to the Bridge of Shadows, an ancient and crumbling structure suspended over an endless abyss. Dark tendrils of magic writhed below, creating an oppressive atmosphere that seemed to weigh on their very souls. "Stay close," Eryndal urged, gripping the amulet tightly. He could feel Emberthane's presence faintly, her magic pulsing like a heartbeat.

As they crossed the bridge, a shadowy figure emerged from the darkness—a Phantom Warden, a guardian bound to the Nexus of ancient magic. Its form was skeletal, wreathed in flickering shadows, and it wielded a blade that seemed to slice through reality itself. The Phantom attacked without hesitation. Its blade moved with terrifying speed, forcing the heroes to work in tandem. Roland absorbed its blows with his shield, while Soren and Eryndal coordinated magical strikes. Aravon, still struggling to fully master his transformations, held back at first, fear flickering in his eyes. When the Phantom's blade struck Roland, sending him sprawling to the ground, Aravon finally acted. Letting out a roar, he transformed again, but this time his movements were deliberate and controlled. He tackled the Phantom, grappling with it until the shadowy figure dissolved into nothingness.

Roland groaned as he sat up, clutching his side. "That's twice now," he muttered, giving Aravon a grudging glance. "Don't let it go to your head."

Aravon smirked, his demonic form fading as he returned to himself. "I'll try."

When the towering spires of Elderion Citadel finally came into view, a wave of relief washed over the group.

Emberthane reappeared, stepping out of the amulet as though emerging from a mist. "You've done well," she said, her voice carrying a rare note of pride.

Chapter 13
Elderion Citadel

The journey to Elderion Citadel had taken its toll on them, but nothing could have prepared the heroes for the sheer majesty awaiting them. The citadel stood as if the mountain itself had willingly shaped its peaks to cradle this ancient fortress. Each spire, impossibly tall, seemed to pierce the heavens, glistening like polished crystal in the soft, perpetual glow that bathed the plateau. The faint hum of ancient magic suffused the air, a tangible reminder of the citadel's power.

The walls of the citadel were an exquisite blend of form and function. The stone shimmered with veins of silver and gold that shifted and moved, alive with ancient energy. Runes etched into the gates pulsed faintly, their glow growing brighter as the group approached. Each rune was a ward, a lock that only those of true purpose and heart could pass. The sheer artistry of the craftsmanship spoke of a time when gods and mortals had worked side by side to build something eternal.

The plateau itself was a marvel. The mountains surrounding Elderion rose like silent sentinels, their jagged peaks softened by the mists that swirled endlessly around them. The air was crisp but carried a warmth that felt protective, almost as if the citadel exuded its own aura to shield those within.

For a moment, none of them spoke. Even Roland, whose scepticism often outweighed his awe, stood silent, his eyes fixed on the massive gates that now loomed before them.

The Arrival of the Imperial Guard

The sudden blaring of horns shattered the stillness, the sound resonating through the mountains like a call to arms. The heroes froze, instinctively reaching for their weapons, but what emerged from the mists was unlike anything they had ever seen.

A dozen figures emerged, their forms both alien and beautiful. The Imperial Guard of Elderion.

Each guard stood tall and commanding, their golden armour gleaming even in the muted light. Their equine lower bodies, sleek and powerful, moved with an elegance that seemed out of place in such massive forms. Their elven upper bodies were regal, their sharp features framed by flowing white hair that shimmered like threads of starlight. Eyes as bright as the sun bore into the group, assessing them with a scrutiny that felt almost physical.

The captain of the guard stepped forward, his armour more elaborate than the others, adorned with a glowing crest that radiated authority. His voice was deep and steady, like the rumble of distant thunder.

"Who dares approach the gates of Elderion Citadel unbidden?"

Eryndal stepped forward, clutching the scroll given to him by Kinzo. His heart pounded in his chest, but his voice was steady. "We come with dire news. The Alliance of the Heart has been reformed, and Raxis's shadow grows once more. We seek the counsel of Elderion."

The captain accepted the scroll, unrolling it with careful hands. His sharp eyes scanned its contents, and for a moment, the air grew still. Finally, he looked back at Eryndal and nodded.

"You will be granted entry. But know this: Elderion's walls have long-guarded secrets that even your dire mission cannot shake."

At his command, the massive gates groaned and creaked, swinging open to reveal the wonders of the citadel within.

The Courtyard: A Living Tapestry

The gates opened into a vast courtyard that seemed to shimmer with life itself. It was as if the very ground beneath their feet pulsed with the heartbeat of the mountain. The cobblestones were inlaid with luminous runes, their soft light shifting as the group walked across them. The runes formed patterns that told stories of ancient battles, alliances forged, and sacrifices made to protect the realm.

Statues of kings and queens stood in solemn lines, each carved with such precision that they seemed ready to step from their pedestals and speak. Their eyes, though stone, held a strange warmth as if they watched over the citadel's visitors with approval or warning.

Waterfalls cascaded from the cliffs above, their water impossibly clear. The streams they fed into wove through the courtyard like veins of silver, forming pools that reflected the sky. These pools teemed with fish that shimmered like gemstones, their scales reflecting every colour imaginable.

The gardens surrounding the pools were unlike any the heroes had ever seen. Flowers bloomed in impossible hues—crimson blossoms that seemed to burn like fire, icy blue petals that shimmered like frost, and golden blooms that hummed softly with a melody only barely audible. Each plant was alive with magic, its energy palpable even to those without the gift of sight.

The Citadel's Heart: Magic Personified

As they moved deeper into the citadel, the sensation of magic grew stronger. The walls seemed alive, their surfaces shifting subtly as if adjusting to the presence of new visitors. Carvings along the corridors depicted scenes of creation: gods and mortals working together to shape the world, forging alliances that had long since passed into legend.

The air itself felt different. It carried a warmth that wasn't physical but emotional as if the citadel was welcoming them yet testing their resolve at the same time. Every sound, from their footsteps to the faint hum of the runes, echoed with a clarity that made it impossible to ignore their presence in this hallowed place.

Roland, who rarely allowed himself to be awed, couldn't hide his astonishment. "This place…it feels alive."

"It is," Eryndal said quietly. "Every stone, every rune—it's all connected. The citadel isn't just a fortress. It's a living archive of our world's history."

The Hall of the Rulers

The path led to the Hall of the Rulers, the citadel's grand throne room. The doors to the hall were massive, carved from a single slab of obsidian inlaid with veins of gold that pulsed like molten fire. Above the doors, an inscription in the Old Tongue read:

Here sit those who bear the weight of eternity.

The guards opened the doors, and the group stepped inside.

The throne room was vast, its ceiling lost in shadow. Pillars of crystal lined the hall, each one glowing faintly and casting fractured light across the polished floor. At the far end of the room stood a single throne, carved from a seamless block of what looked like starlight frozen in time. Behind the throne, a massive stained-glass window depicted the creation of the world, its colours shifting subtly as if the scene were alive.

No one sat upon the throne.

Instead, the hall was filled with an ethereal presence. It was as if the room itself was watching them, waiting to hear their purpose.

The Guardians of Knowledge

As the group approached the throne, figures began to emerge from the shadows. They were the Guardians of Knowledge, the keepers of Elderion's secrets. Each wore flowing robes that shimmered like liquid silver, and their faces were obscured by hoods. Their voices, when they spoke, resonated as if a thousand years of wisdom echoed within each word.

"You have come to Elderion seeking answers," one of the guardians said, their tone neither welcoming nor hostile. "But know this: the answers you seek are not without cost."

Eryndal stepped forward, bowing his head. "We seek to understand the nature of Raxis's power and how we might defeat him. The Alliance of the Heart has been reformed, but without the knowledge held within these walls, we are doomed to repeat the mistakes of the past."

The guardians exchanged glances, their movements fluid and deliberate. Finally, the one who had spoken nodded. "Very well. You will be allowed access to the archives. But be warned: the knowledge you uncover may test your resolve and your unity."

The Path Beneath the Citadel

The group was led to a hidden passage beneath the throne room, a spiral staircase that seemed to descend into the very heart of the mountain. The air grew colder as they descended, and the faint hum of magic was replaced by an almost deafening silence.

The walls of the passage were carved with ancient symbols that even Eryndal couldn't decipher. Soren ran her fingers along the carvings, her expression thoughtful. "These are older than anything I've ever seen. Older than the gods, even."

At the bottom of the staircase, they emerged into a cavernous chamber filled with rows upon rows of crystalline tablets. The light from their torches refracted off the crystals, casting rainbows across the walls.

Eryndal approached one of the tablets, his fingers brushing its surface. The moment he touched it, the crystal flared to life, projecting images and sounds into the air. It was a memory, preserved in perfect detail—a battle between the gods and a monstrous entity that could only be Raxis.

"This," Eryndal whispered, "is what we need."

The Weight of Knowledge

As the group explored the archives, they uncovered more than just the history of Raxis. They learned of the sacrifices made by the original Alliance of the Heart, of the betrayal that had nearly doomed them all, and of the true cost of wielding the power necessary to defeat the darkness.

The citadel, for all its beauty, was a reminder of the fragile balance between creation and destruction. And as the heroes delved deeper into its secrets, they couldn't shake the feeling that they were being watched—not by the guardians or the citadel itself, but by something far older, waiting in the shadows for its moment to strike.

The Elderion Citadel was more than a fortress. It was a crucible, a place where heroes were tested, and the fate of the world was decided. A guardian appeared from the shadows, "Eryndal, Soren, Roland and Aravon, you have been summoned to the grand hall of Elderion. Please, if you will, follow me."

Secrets Unveiled: Truths of Blood and Power

The grand hall of Elderion was a place that demanded reverence. Its vaulted ceilings soared high above, an expanse of artistry that seemed to capture the very heavens. Thousands of glowing crystals were suspended from the ceiling, their light forming intricate constellations that shifted subtly as if alive. Each star seemed to pulse with an inner energy, casting a soft luminescence that bathed the hall in an ethereal glow.

Beneath the cosmic canopy, the heroes stood on polished marble floors that reflected the celestial patterns above. Encircling them were the council of kings and queens, representatives of every race and kingdom of Reldad. Their presence was both regal and humbling, their ornate attire and majestic crowns reflecting centuries of tradition and power.

At the centre of the council stood the High Sovereign, her silver hair flowing like liquid moonlight, her piercing blue eyes holding the weight of countless decisions made for the good of the realm. Her crown was understated compared to the others—made of white gold, with a single brilliant sapphire—but its simplicity only amplified her commanding presence.

When Eryndal finished recounting their journey and the confirmation of Raxis's return, silence descended over the hall like a heavy shroud.

The High Sovereign's Warning

The High Sovereign broke the silence, her voice carrying the clarity of a bell yet weighted with foreboding.

"If Raxis rises again," she said, "the secrets of this citadel will be both our salvation and our undoing."

Her words hung in the air, and at her subtle gesture, an elder sorcerer from the Magisterium stepped forward. The sorcerer's robes of gold and green shimmered with threads of enchantment, their fabric seeming to shift between cloth and light. His hair was white, his beard long and meticulously braided, and his pale green eyes glowed faintly with latent magic.

"There is much you do not know, heroes," he began, his voice a mixture of tremor and authority. "Your journey has brought you to truths that have been hidden for centuries—truths not only about this realm but about yourselves."

The Revelation

The sorcerer's words were met with puzzled glances from the group. Aravon, who had remained silent throughout their audience, now looked between them, his young face reflecting both curiosity and unease.

The elder's gaze swept over the three heroes: Eryndal, Soren, and Roland. His eyes lingered on each of them as if seeing not their physical forms but something deeper, something hidden within.

"Eryndal Bethkalen. Soren Dalithian. Roland Bardin," he said, pronouncing their names with a weight that made each syllable feel like a revelation. "You share more than a common goal. You share blood."

A gasp rippled through the hall.

"Each of you," the sorcerer continued, "is a child of Lord Thalion Bethkalen, a man who once walked these halls as a trusted advisor, as one of the most powerful sorcerers the world has ever known."

Disbelief and Questions

Eryndal staggered back a step, his mind reeling. His voice, usually so composed, cracked with disbelief. "But that cannot be. My father was a simple man—a teacher, nothing more."

The sorcerer's faint smile was tinged with both amusement and sadness. "Thalion was many things, child. A teacher, yes, but also a warrior, a diplomat, and above all, a sorcerer of unmatched power. He wielded magic that could bend the very fabric of existence. And it was he who first forged the Alliance of the Heart."

Soren's face, usually calm and unyielding, now betrayed her inner turmoil. "My mother never spoke of him," she murmured. "She told me my father was…lost."

"Not lost," the sorcerer corrected gently. "Hidden. For reasons you are only now beginning to uncover."

Roland's fists clenched tightly at his sides, his voice hard with bitterness. "Then why did he leave us? Why did he abandon us to walk separate paths, never knowing each other?"

The elder sorcerer's expression darkened, the faint glow in his eyes dimming. "Because he knew the truth of his own bloodline."

The room seemed to hold its breath as the sorcerer spoke the next words.

"Lord Thalion Bethkalen was not merely a sorcerer. He was the brother of Raxis."

The Weight of Truth

The revelation fell like a thunderclap. The constellations above seemed to dim as if even the crystals themselves were stunned by the gravity of the words.

Eryndal was the first to recover his voice, though it trembled with emotion. "You mean to say…we are kin to the darkness we fight against?"

"Yes," the sorcerer confirmed. "Thalion and Raxis were born of the same blood, though they could not have been more different in purpose. While Thalion sought to unite the realms through knowledge and harmony, Raxis craved dominion and power. Their conflict is what shattered the original Alliance of the Heart and nearly destroyed this world."

Soren's hand went instinctively to the hilt of her blade, her knuckles white as she gripped it tightly. "Why were we never told? Why keep this from us?"

The High Sovereign stepped forward, her expression softening with sympathy. "Because knowledge of your bloodline is both a gift and a curse. To know that you share the blood of both the world's saviour and its destroyer, it could break even the strongest of spirits."

Roland's voice was sharp, his anger barely contained. "And yet you chose to tell us now when the enemy we face is stronger than ever? What do you expect us to do with this knowledge?"

"To use it," the High Sovereign said firmly. "The blood you carry is a bond, a tether to power that only you can wield. Raxis may be your enemy, but he is also your kin. That connection may be the key to his undoing—or to your own."

The Magisterium's Insight

The elder sorcerer gestured, and the air in front of him shimmered as he conjured an image. It was a memory, a fragment of the past preserved in magic. The group saw a younger Thalion and Raxis, their resemblance striking. Thalion's face was noble and kind, his eyes filled with wisdom, while Raxis's features were sharp, his gaze burning with ambition.

"They were inseparable once," the sorcerer said. "Brothers bound by love and loyalty. But as they grew, so too did their differences. Thalion sought to protect the balance of the world, while Raxis sought to rule it. Their conflict was inevitable."

The image shifted, showing a great battle between the brothers. Thalion wielded magic that seemed to flow like water, adaptable and harmonious. Raxis's power, by contrast, was raw and destructive, a fire that consumed everything it touched.

"Their final confrontation shattered the first Alliance," the sorcerer continued. "Thalion believed he had sealed Raxis away forever, but even he could not destroy his brother completely. That task, it seems, has fallen to you."

The Weight of Destiny

The heroes stood in silence, the enormity of their heritage settling over them like a storm. Each of them grappled with the implications of the revelation.

Eryndal, who had always seen himself as a humble mage, now bore the weight of a legacy he had never asked for.

Soren, whose strength had always been her anchor, felt the foundations of her identity shaken.

Roland, ever the sceptic, struggled to reconcile the anger he felt towards a father he never knew with the undeniable truth of his bloodline.

And Aravon, the boy who had suffered so much at the hands of his own family, watched them with a mixture of sympathy and fear.

The High Sovereign spoke again, her voice gentle but resolute. "You have a choice to make. You can embrace this truth and use it to forge a new path, or you can let it consume you as it once consumed Thalion and Raxis. The fate of this world depends on your decision."

A New Purpose

The council granted the heroes the night to reflect, offering them the sanctuary of Elderion's sacred walls. As they walked through the citadel's gardens, their hearts heavy with the weight of what they had learned, they found themselves drawn together in a way they hadn't been before.

Eryndal was the first to speak, his voice quiet but firm. "We may share blood with Raxis, but that does not define who we are. We have a chance to end this, to succeed where Thalion failed."

Soren nodded, her grip on her blade steady once more. "Our bloodline may be a curse, but it's also a gift. If Thalion could stand against Raxis, then so can we."

Roland sighed, his usual sarcasm absent. "I never wanted any of this, but if we're the only ones who can stop him, then I'm not walking away."

Aravon, his voice soft but determined, added, "You're not like them. You've already proven that. And maybe…maybe that's why you're the ones who can win."

In that moment, the heroes found a renewed sense of purpose. They were no longer just adventurers or outcasts. They were heirs to a legacy of both darkness and light, and they would use that legacy to forge a new future for Reldad. They decided they didn't need the night to reflect, their decision was made and final.

As they returned to the grand hall, the High Sovereign and the council awaited them, their expressions expectant.

Eryndal stepped forward, his voice clear and unwavering. "We will not let our bloodline define us. We will use it to end Raxis's reign once and for all."

The High Sovereign smiled; her eyes gleaming with approval. "Then the Alliance of the Heart is truly reborn. May your strength and unity guide us all."

And so, with the weight of their newfound truth upon them, the heroes set forth on the next chapter of their journey, their resolve stronger than ever. The secrets of Elderion had been unveiled, and with them, the hope of a world on the brink of ruin.

Chapter 14
The Keys of Elderion

The air in the grand hall of Elderion was heavy with the echoes of their oath. The High Sovereign's approving gaze lingered on the group for a moment longer before she turned to the elder sorcerer. Her voice, sharp yet composed, cut through the lingering silence.

"Then it is decided. The Alliance of the Heart is reborn," she said. "But words alone will not carry you through the trials ahead. There is much you must learn, and Elderion holds the knowledge you require."

The elder sorcerer stepped forward once more, his faintly glowing eyes flickering towards the vaulted ceiling of constellations. He spoke with gravity. "Your bloodlines grant you strength, but they also bind you to the destiny of this world. Elderion was once the heart of that destiny, and within its walls lie the tools that can aid you in your quest—if you are strong enough to claim them."

The Sacred Vaults

The group was led out of the grand hall, escorted by the regal, half-elven Imperial Guard. Their hooves echoed against the polished marble floors, each strike resonating with the magic imbued in the very foundation of the citadel. Soren kept her hand near her sword, her instincts wary despite the guard's apparent allegiance. Eryndal, meanwhile, couldn't tear his eyes away from the murals lining the corridors they passed through.

The walls were alive with art, depicting events and figures from Reldad's history. Massive reliefs carved into shimmering stone told the tale of the First Age when the gods had walked alongside mortals. Other panels showed the creation of the Imperial Guard and the establishment of Elderion Citadel as a bastion against the forces of chaos.

The further they travelled, the more the artwork shifted. The images became darker and more chaotic. They passed depictions of battles so violent and destructive that even the masterful carvings seemed to tremble with residual energy. Aravon paused at one mural, his eyes fixed on the central figure.

"Raxis," he murmured, his voice barely audible.

The tyrant sorcerer was carved into the stone with terrifying detail, his outstretched hands unleashing rivers of fire and shadow that consumed entire armies. Behind him loomed monstrous figures—abominations of bone, sinew, and dark magic.

"Keep moving," Roland urged, his tone unusually curt.

The group finally reached an immense set of double doors, made from a gleaming black stone veined with gold. The runes etched into the surface pulsed with an ancient magic that seemed to hum in harmony with the air itself.

"This," said the elder sorcerer, "is the entrance to the Sacred Vaults of Elderion. Within lies relics and knowledge sealed away since the fall of the First Alliance. But be warned—the vaults do not yield their secrets easily."

The Trial of the Vaults

At the sorcerer's command, the runes on the doors flared to life, and the doors began to part with a low, resonant groan. A wave of cold air rushed out, carrying with it the scent of ancient stone and forgotten magic.

Beyond the doors was a vast, circular chamber that stretched into darkness. The walls were lined with towering shelves and pedestals, each holding objects cloaked in faint, shimmering light. The air was thick with enchantments, and the faint hum of ancient spells vibrated beneath their feet.

The elder sorcerer turned to the group. "The vaults are not merely a repository of knowledge. They are alive, bound by the will of Elderion itself. Only those deemed worthy can claim what lies within."

Eryndal furrowed his brow. "What does 'worthy' mean?"

The sorcerer smiled faintly. "That is for the vaults to decide."

As soon as they stepped inside, the doors slammed shut behind them, and the runes on the walls flared. A deep, resonant voice filled the chamber, emanating from everywhere and nowhere.

Seekers of Elderion, you stand before the Heart of the Realm. Prove your purpose or be consumed by your doubt.

The First Challenge: The Hall of Mirrors

The air shifted, and the chamber transformed around them. The towering shelves dissolved, replaced by an endless expanse of mirrors. Each mirror reflected the group, but the reflections were distorted—twisted versions of themselves that flickered between light and shadow.

"What is this?" Soren whispered, her voice tense.

"A test," Eryndal replied, his voice tinged with awe.

The mirrors began to ripple, and the distorted reflections stepped out, taking on physical form. Each one bore the face of a hero but moved with an unnatural, jerking gait. They raised weapons forged of shadow and lunged.

The fight that followed was chaotic and desperate. Roland faced off against a version of himself whose movements were impossibly fast, forcing him to rely on instinct rather than precision. Soren clashed with her double, whose blade seemed to anticipate her every strike.

Eryndal's battle was less physical but no less harrowing. His reflection conjured spells that mirrored his own, forcing him to confront his deepest fears: his doubts about his own power and his ability to lead.

It was Aravon who ultimately turned the tide. As the others struggled, he stood in the centre of the chaos, his small form radiating determination.

"Enough!" he shouted.

The voice of the vault responded. **"Do you see the truth, child of shadow and light?"**

"I see it," Aravon said, his voice steady. "We are not defined by our reflections. We are more than what we fear."

The mirrored versions froze, then dissolved into mist. The chamber shifted once more, and the group found themselves back in the circular room.

The Second Challenge: The Veil of Memories

Before they could catch their breath, the room shifted again. This time, they found themselves in a dimly lit corridor lined with tapestries. As they walked, the tapestries began to move, their threads weaving and unweaving to depict scenes from their pasts.

Eryndal saw himself as a child, studying magic under his father's patient guidance. But the image darkened, showing his father's sudden departure, leaving him with unanswered questions and a growing sense of inadequacy.

Soren's tapestry depicted her life as a warrior, her victories on the battlefield juxtaposed with the loneliness of her upbringing. The faces of comrades lost in battle stared back at her, their silent gazes filled with accusation.

Roland's memories were the harshest of all. He saw himself as a child, struggling to survive in a world that seemed to care nothing for him. He saw betrayal and heartbreak, his own choices leaving scars that never truly healed.

The corridor seemed endless, each step forcing them to confront their failures, their regrets, and their fears.

"It's a trick," Roland growled, his voice raw with emotion. "They're trying to break us."

"No," Eryndal said quietly. "They're trying to remind us."

"Of what?" Soren asked, her voice tight.

"Of who we are," Eryndal replied. "Of what we've overcome to be here."

With those words, the corridor began to fade, and the group emerged into the circular chamber once more.

The Third Challenge: The Relics of Power

The final challenge was unlike the others. The air in the chamber grew still, and the shimmering objects on the pedestals seemed to call out to them, their light pulsing in time with the beating of their hearts.

"Choose wisely," the voice of the vault intoned.

Eryndal approached a pedestal bearing a staff of pure crystal. As his fingers closed around it, the staff pulsed with energy, and he felt a surge of power, unlike anything he had ever known. The voice spoke again.

The Staff of Veledan, forged by the first magi. May it guide you through the shadows.

Soren's gaze fell upon a shield adorned with a phoenix emblem. When she touched it, the metal flared with a fiery light, and she felt an unshakeable sense of resolve.

The Shield of Cindralis, protector of the fallen. May it grant you the strength to endure.

Roland hesitated before selecting a dagger with a blade of obsidian. It seemed to hum in his hand, its edge sharper than any mortal weapon.

The Fang of Kaelthar, born of the night. May it strike true against the darkness.

Even Aravon was not left out. A small amulet in the shape of a crescent moon glowed softly as he lifted it, its warmth filling him with a sense of hope.

The Amulet of Ilven; light of the lost. May it guide your path.

The Journey Ahead

With the relics claimed, the vault's voice spoke one final time.

You have proven your worth. Go forth, heirs of the Alliance, and may the light of Elderion guide you.

The doors opened, and the group stepped out into the light of the citadel once more. The High Sovereign and the council awaited them, their expressions filled with quiet expectation.

"You have claimed the keys of Elderion," the High Sovereign said. "But your journey is far from over. Thalion is dead, and his legacy rests with you now. Use it wisely."

Eryndal nodded, his grip tightening on the staff. "We will."

As they left the great hall, the weight of their new purpose settled over them. They were no longer just adventurers or outcasts. They were the heirs of a forgotten legacy, and their fight against Raxis had truly begun.

Chapter 15
The Fall of Aetherion

In the quiet aftermath of their harrowing journey, the heroes sat by the warmth of the campfire, their thoughts heavy with revelation. Emberthane's ethereal glow flickered faintly in the dim light as she pieced together the truth that tied them all to a shared lineage. "You are not just brothers and sisters," Emberthane began, her tone careful but firm. "Your father, Thalipon Bethkalen, was the brother of Raxis himself. By blood, you are kin to the darkness that now threatens Reldad."

Eryndal clenched his jaw, his hand instinctively brushing against his wounded side as if to distract himself. Roland remained silent, staring into the fire, his brows furrowed in thought. Soren, ever the mediator, broke the silence. "If this is true," she said softly, "then we are also kin to Aravon, Raxis' son." Emberthane nodded.

"The blood of Thalion and Raxis runs through you all. It explains your gifts, your shared connection to magic, and your ties to each other. But it also explains why Raxis may view you as his greatest threat—or his greatest weapon." The words hung heavy, casting a shadow over the camp.

The fire's glow danced against the dense canopy of trees above the heroes' camp, but the light brought no warmth to their sombre faces. Emberthane's words lingered in the air like the echo of distant thunder. Even the crackling flames seemed subdued as if the weight of the revelation had smothered their usual vitality.

Her tone was grave as she continued, each syllable laced with a dire urgency. "Morva Sable's ambitions are greater than even Raxis's return. She hunts the Elder Scrolls—ancient texts of untold power, scattered and hidden to prevent them from ever being read in unison. Together, these scrolls reveal the locations of the four shards, the pillars of the old magics that sustained the balance of our world. If she unites them, Raxis will not simply return—he will ascend to a godlike power that none can oppose."

The weight of her words pressed down on them all.

Eryndal was the first to speak, his voice sharp with unease. "She already has one, doesn't she?"

Emberthane nodded solemnly. "The Shard of Obsidian. It is the key to her current power and the reason why she is so much more dangerous than even the tales suggest. The Shard contains an ancient, malevolent force—a power she has bound to herself."

Soren leaned forward; her brows furrowed in deep thought. "What kind of power?"

"A name you've likely only heard in whispers," Emberthane said. "Saelvira Nox."

Saelvira Nox: The Witch Queen

The mention of Saelvira Nox cast a chill over the camp, as though the Witch Queen's shadow had fallen over them from afar.

Roland, ever the pragmatist, scoffed nervously. "Saelvira Nox? That's just a name mothers use to frighten their children. A bedtime story, nothing more."

"No," Emberthane said sharply, her eyes narrowing. "She is no mere tale. Saelvira Nox is real, and her return is a harbinger of despair. She ruled over Nyxalon centuries ago, a kingdom consumed by shadow and death. Her power was unmatched, and her influence spread like a plague across the lands of Reldad. The Magisterium and the Alliance of the Heart united to banish her, but even then, it took everything they had. The Shard of Obsidian was her prison, a fragment of her essence bound to keep her spirit contained. By wielding the Shard, Morva has given Saelvira form once more."

Eryndal's expression darkened. "You're saying Morva has resurrected her? That she's…alive?"

"Alive, yes in every sense of the word," Emberthane replied. "Saelvira Nox's body was never destroyed, it was buried along with thousands of others in the Blackwater Marshes, her soul attached to one of the shards. Her soul grows stronger with each moment she remains bound to the Shard. Through Morva, she walks the mortal realm again, her influence seeping into every corner of Reldad."

The Witch Queen's Dominion

The tales of Saelvira Nox were as ancient as they were terrifying. The Witch Queen's rise had been sudden, and her reign of terror swift. She had discovered the forbidden arts long before the Magisterium had codified their laws. Her power, it was said, did not come from the gods but from the void—a plane of existence beyond the reach of light and order.

As Emberthane recounted her deeds, the firelight seemed to flicker ominously, as though the forest itself recoiled from her words. "Saelvira was no ordinary sorceress. She bent life and death to her will, raising armies of the dead and twisting living creatures into monstrous abominations. But her most fearsome power was her ability to corrupt the minds of those who opposed her. Even the purest of hearts could be turned to darkness under her influence."

"She doesn't just kill," Soren said grimly, her hand tightening around the hilt of her sword. "She destroys everything a person is."

Emberthane nodded. "And with Morva at her side, she is more dangerous than ever. Together, they are an unstoppable force, a storm that threatens to consume us all."

The Battle for Aetherion

The floating city of Aetherion, a marvel of ancient sorcery and craftsmanship, hung suspended in the heavens, its spires glimmering like diamonds against the endless night. Rivers of light flowed through its streets, and its towers hummed with the power of the Magisterium. Yet, on this night, that light was dimmed by a shadow more profound than any the city had known.

Descending upon Aetherion like a storm came Morva Sable and her ally, the Witch Queen Saelvira Nox. Morva stood resplendent in the dark power of the Shard of Obsidian, its unholy aura surrounding her in a halo of pure malice. Her presence was a command, her form a silhouette of cruelty and ambition. Beside her, Saelvira was a nightmare brought to life. Her elongated figure was draped in shredded robes that seemed to absorb the light around her, her claw-like hands radiating a faint green glow. Saelvira's eyes—two orbs of sickly luminescence—pierced through the air like beacons of terror.

Her voice, when she spoke, carried a haunting melody that sent shivers through the souls of those who heard it. It wasn't merely sound—it was a presence that invaded thoughts, turning courage into despair.

The Hounds of Doom followed close behind. Twisted creatures born of arcane corruption, they were Morva's brutal vanguard. They prowled on all fours yet shifted unnaturally into grotesque humanoid shapes when they struck. Their fur shimmered with an oily iridescence, and their claws glowed with runes of forbidden magic. Each step they took left scorch marks on the pristine pathways of Aetherion.

As the invading force reached the city's gates, its defenders readied themselves. Kaldrith Greystone, leader of the loyalist Magisterium sorcerers, stood at the forefront, his staff glowing with runes of defiance. Around him were the last bastions of Aetherion's faithful: Maradyn Aevor, whose fiery hair seemed to mirror her mastery of flame; Berrik Fenhallow, a stoic master of defensive wards; and Selithra Valen, ethereal and ghostly, her magic tied to the winds and unseen forces. Together, they commanded the full power of Aetherion's ancient wards.

The First Clash

The battle erupted with terrifying ferocity. The Hounds of Doom surged forward, their howls splitting the air like thunder. As they clashed with Aetherion's defenders, the streets became a maelstrom of destruction.

Kaldrith led the charge, his staff sweeping arcs of white fire that scorched the front line of the Hounds. Maradyn stood beside him, unleashing waves of molten flame that set the ground ablaze, forcing the creatures to recoil. Berrik raised shimmering shields of light to protect the loyalists, while Selithra's spectral winds threw enemies into disarray, scattering them like leaves in a tempest.

But for every hound slain, two more seemed to take its place, their unholy forms rising again through the corruptive magic binding them to Morva's will.

Then came the true devastation. Morva Sable strode into the fray, the Shard of Obsidian blazing against her chest. With a single gesture, she unleashed waves of energy that tore through Aetherion's defences. Walls of stone disintegrated, and magical wards crumbled as if they were paper.

Kaldrith faced her, his voice ringing with defiance. "You betray the very magic you claim to command, Morva! Aetherion will not fall to your treachery!"

But Morva only laughed, a cold, venomous sound. "Aetherion's power was never meant for cowards like you, Kaldrith. You hoard its secrets while the world crumbles. I will remake this world in my image, and your city will be the first to burn."

Saelvira Nox joined the fray then, her presence turning the tide of battle entirely. With a flick of her clawed fingers, she bent reality itself. Spells cast by the defenders unravelled midair, their carefully woven magic dissolving into sparks. Selithra tried to summon a gust of wind to repel the Witch Queen, but Saelvira countered effortlessly, twisting the wind into a spiralling vortex that threw the sorceress into a crumbling tower.

Maradyn screamed in rage, hurling a fireball the size of a boulder towards Saelvira. The Witch Queen absorbed the attack with her outstretched hand, the flames snuffed out in a puff of dark smoke.

"You are but children playing with fire," Saelvira sneered, her voice echoing unnaturally. "And I am the darkness that consumes it."

The City Crumbles

Despite their courage and resolve, the defenders of Aetherion were no match for the combined might of Morva and Saelvira. The spires of the city, once so radiant and untouchable, began to collapse under the relentless assault. The floating bridges that connected the towers shattered, sending fragments of stone and shimmering light cascading into the abyss below.

Kaldrith, battered and bloodied, rallied the remaining defenders at the Hall of Light, Aetherion's most sacred chamber. Its walls were lined with ancient runes of protection, and its central altar contained a shard of pure starlight—one of the city's most potent sources of power.

The Betrayal of the Magisterium

For centuries, Aetherion had been a symbol of hope and stability, its halls home to the most learned sorcerers in the realm. But even within its shimmering walls, darkness had taken root.

The Magisterium was governed by twelve sorcerers, each a master of their respective discipline and sworn to uphold the balance of the world. Yet that balance had been fractured. Morva Sable's influence had wormed its way into the city, her seductive promises of power and immortality tempting many to betray their sacred oaths.

Of the twelve, eight had succumbed. These traitors, now known as the Shadowed Council, had pledged themselves to Morva, their once-brilliant magic now twisted and corrupted. Their loyalty to the Magisterium was gone, replaced by a fervent desire to see Morva's vision realised.

The Loyalists' Last Stand

The remaining four members of the Magisterium, led by the venerable Kaldrith Greystone, had refused to yield. Kaldrith, a sorcerer of immense power and unshakeable conviction, had spent decades guarding the Magisterium's secrets. Now, he stood as the last line of defence against the Shadowed Council.

Within the Hall of Light, the loyalists made their stand. The chamber, once a place of meditation and enlightenment, had been fortified into a bastion. Its walls shimmered with protective wards, and its central dais was surrounded by a web of intricate runes designed to repel dark magic.

Kaldrith addressed his comrades, his voice calm but resolute. "The Shadowed Council has turned Aetherion into a den of vipers, but they have not yet claimed the city's soul. As long as we hold this hall, there is hope. Morva may possess the Shard, but we have something she does not—time. The Elder Scrolls are hidden, and without them, her plans remain incomplete."

His words were met with murmurs of agreement, but the tension in the room was palpable. The loyalists knew they were outnumbered, their magic dwarfed by the combined power of the Shadowed Council.

The Siege of Aetherion

In the Hall of Light, Kaldrith and his comrades fought valiantly, their combined magic forming a barrier that held the enemy at bay. Yet for every spell they cast, the Shadowed Council countered with twice the force. The air crackled with energy, the clash of arcane power shaking the very foundations of the city.

Kaldrith's voice rang out above the chaos. "Hold the line! If we falter, Aetherion will fall, and with it, the last hope for Reldad."

His words galvanised the loyalists, their determination burning brighter even as their strength waned. But the Shadowed Council was relentless. Their spells grew darker, more insidious, as they called upon forbidden magics to break through the hall's defences.

But their defiance was short-lived.

Morva and Saelvira approached the hall with deliberate steps, their forces parting to let them pass. Morva's voice rang out, a taunting melody.

"Surrender, Kaldrith. You cannot hope to defeat me. Your city is mine, your power is mine. All that remains is your submission."

Kaldrith raised his staff, his voice steady despite the odds. "You may claim victory here, Morva, but you will not claim us. We will not be your pawns."

The Final Spell

As Morva and Saelvira unleashed their combined power, the defenders responded with a desperate gambit. Kaldrith, Maradyn, Berrik, and Selithra joined hands, their voices rising in unison as they chanted an ancient incantation. The runes of the Hall of Light began to glow, and the shard of starlight on the altar blazed with an intensity that rivalled the sun.

The spell was not one of victory but of escape. Kaldrith knew that the battle was lost, but the knowledge they carried—the truths about the Elder Scrolls and the amulets—had to survive. As the spell reached its crescendo, a dome of radiant light enveloped the four sorcerers, shielding them from Morva's onslaught.

Morva screamed in frustration, hurling bolts of dark energy at the dome, but it held firm. Saelvira watched with cold amusement, her clawed hand resting lightly on Morva's shoulder. "Let them flee," she said, her voice dripping with malice. "Their escape only delays the inevitable."

With a final burst of light, the four sorcerers vanished, leaving the ruins of Aetherion behind.

Escape to the Citadel

A sense of relative peace had settled over the group as they sat around the campfire, the flickering flames casting long shadows against the citadel's imposing walls. The night air was cool, filled with the scent of the moss-covered stone, and the only sounds were the occasional crackle from the fire and the distant rustle of wind in the trees. But that peaceful moment was shattered by a deafening bang that echoed through the citadel like a thunderclap. The ground trembled beneath them, and the fire flared brightly, casting a stark, brief light over the surroundings. The noise seemed to come from the grand hall—the heart of the citadel. Almost as if on instinct, the heroes immediately sprang to their feet, weapons drawn and eyes alert.

"What in the name of the gods was that?" Soren asked, her voice steady despite the surprise, her hand resting on the hilt of her blade. Eryndal was already moving, his senses on high alert. He clutched the amulet that Emberthane had entrusted to him, the weight of it suddenly feeling heavier as if it sensed the approaching danger. "Magic, ancient, powerful magic," he murmured, his voice low, his eyes narrowing towards the citadel's darkened silhouette.

Before anyone could respond, the air seemed to shimmer, followed by a blinding flash of light that erupted from the grand hall, spilling out through the high-arched windows of the citadel. The light illuminated the surroundings in unnatural colours—golden and crimson hues danced across the walls, like the reflection of a storm's fury on the horizon.

The sharp sound of the citadel's great bell began to toll— its deep, resonant chimes echoing across the night air, a signal of alarm. The heroes instinctively began to move towards the sound, but before they could make a move, the gates of the citadel swung open with a groan, and the Centauri Guards poured out, their majestic, half-horse, half-elf forms silhouetted against the light. Their armour gleamed in the flash, and their spears were raised in a defensive position.

"Protect the Sovereign!" the Centauri commander barked, eyes scanning the horizon for threats, "All others stand back."

Despite the command, Eryndal, Sore, Roland and Aravon pushed forward. Emberthane retreated into the amulet. Their shared urgency drove them to uncover the source of the disturbance. They moved swiftly through the citadel's courtyard, past guards who saluted them but did not dare impede their progress. The grand hall was just ahead, the towering double doors cracked open, revealing an intense light swirling from within. As the heroes entered the hall, they were met with the shocking sight of four familiar figures.

The sorcerers had reappeared within the halls of Elderion Citadel, their bodies battered and their spirits weary. The transition left them sprawled on the cold marble floor, gasping for breath. The once-pristine robes of the Magisterium were torn and scorched, their magical reserves nearly depleted.

Kaldrith was the first to rise, leaning heavily on his staff. His green eyes burned with urgency as he addressed the heroes who had gathered to meet them.

"Aetherion has fallen," he said, his voice hoarse but resolute. "Eight of our brothers and sisters have turned to Morva's side. They have joined her Shadowed Council, and now she commands not only the Hounds of Doom but the Witch Queen Saelvira Nox herself. The Shard of Obsidian grants her power we cannot comprehend."

Maradyn, her fiery hair singed and her face streaked with ash stepped forward. "We fought with everything we had, but it wasn't enough. The city is lost, and the Elder Scrolls are now in greater danger than ever. If Morva gathers them all, she will find the remaining amulets and awaken Raxis."

Selithra, her voice ethereal and soft, added, "The Hounds are a plague upon this world. Their very presence corrupts all it touches. And Saelvira's power..." She shuddered. "It is unlike anything we've faced before."

The heroes listened in stunned silence, their faces pale as the magnitude of the threat sank in.

The Heroes' Resolve

Eryndal clenched his fists, his knuckles white with tension. "Then we stop her," he said, his voice filled with determination. "If Morva finds the Elder Scrolls, it's over. We have to act now—before she gathers more power."

Roland, his hand resting on the hilt of his blade, nodded grimly. "We've seen what she's capable of, and we know what's at stake. If Aetherion wasn't safe, then nowhere is. We have to move quickly."

Soren placed a hand on Eryndal's shoulder, her voice calm but firm. "We have the blood of Thalion. The Alliance of the Heart was forged to face threats like this. We've stood against darkness before, and we will again."

Kaldrith stepped closer, his eyes locking with Eryndal's. "You are our last hope. The amulets must be found before Morva claims them. The balance of the world depends on it. Will you rise to the challenge?"

Eryndal met his gaze, a fire igniting in his heart. "We will. For Aetherion. For the Magisterium. For all of Reldad."

As the first mournful howls of the hounds echoed in the distance, the heroes prepared themselves for the battles to come. Darkness had descended upon the world, but they knew they were the light that could break it.